NOW I LAY ME DOWN TO SLEEP

HARLAN HAGUE

WOLFPACK
PUBLISHING
— EST 2013 —

Now I Lay Me Down To Sleep
Paperback Edition
Copyright © 2022 Harlan Hague

Published in the United States by Wolfpack Publishing, Las Vegas.

Wolfpack Publishing
9850 S. Maryland Parkway, Suite A-5 #323
Las Vegas, Nevada 89183

wolfpackpublishing.com

Paperback ISBN 978-1-63977-815-7
eBook ISBN 978-1-63977-816-4
LCCN 2022947678

Now I Lay Me Down
To Sleep

There is no history, only fictions of varying degrees of plausibility.
—Voltaire

CHAPTER 1

Professor Brett Davis stood at an open window of the second-story classroom, hands in pockets. He stared at the leafy canopy in the line of oaks, shimmering in the light breeze.

A full minute passed. Students in the packed stair-stepped room looked aside at each other, waiting. The only sound was the soft flutter of leaves in the canopy. Students began to fidget, frowning, whispering.

A girl in the front row leaned forward in her chair. "Uh, Doctor Davis?" The other students looked down at her. Some grinned. Everyone in the classroom but the professor knew Gilly had a fierce crush on him. Dr. Davis indeed was handsome, the youngest full professor in the faculty. At thirty-eight, he looked younger. And he appeared the proper younger professor, dressed in jeans and button-down collar shirt, cuffs turned up.

He turned to face the class. "The point is..." He stopped, turned aside. He looked back to the class. "The point is... we have spent the better part of the semester doing what?"

Students looked again at each other, some frowning, some slumped in their chairs. "I got the impression that we're studying history," said Benjamin from his chair in the back row. A few nervous snickers.

"So we are," said Professor Davis. "By the way, Benjamin, what is history?"

Benjamin straightened. "Well, history is what happened. We study what happened."

"Do we now?" Davis rubbed his chin. "How do we know what happened?"

Benjamin frowned. "Well, we know what happened by reading books, accounts written by people who were there or who have researched what happened and wrote it down. And by listening to you." Scattered chuckles.

"Okay," said Davis, "but what—"

Suddenly the classroom hall door flew open. There stood a disheveled man, wearing a shirt two sizes too large, badly tucked into baggy trousers, long hair flying in all directions. "Come out here, Brett, I need to talk to you. Now." He glared at the professor.

Davis stared at the interloper who held the door wide open. "I can't come now, man. I have a class."

"You said you'd come!" He shook his fist, his face angry. "You're a loser!" He slammed the door shut.

Silence. Students looked at each other. "What th' hell was that all about?" said Benjamin softly to no one in particular. There was a low conversational buzz in the room.

"Okay, look at me and listen up," said Davis. "Take out a single sheet of paper, quickly, quickly." He spoke rapidly. "Describe this man, this intruder. What was he wearing? Colors, styles. How old was he? Was he calm or agitated? What did he say? Verbatim, please. What did he do? Did he stand in the doorway, or did he step inside? Describe his appearance, face, hair, manner. What did I say to him? You have three minutes."

Students looked at Davis, then at each other, confused. They didn't move.

"C'mon, c'mon. Get busy. You have only three minutes. Don't put your name on the paper. Just write. Quickly, quickly."

The class suddenly was in motion. Students found paper and pen, bent over their papers and wrote. Some worked on cellphones and iPads. They paused, wrote, looked at the ceiling, wrote, looked at the window, wrote.

Davis watched his cellphone. After three minutes, he raised an arm, said: "Enough, pens down." Students put pens and phones down, most frowning, glancing aside at each other, still confused, some visibly upset.

"Right. Now," said Davis, "what color was his shirt?"

Students tensed, but seemed eager to get on with it, whatever "it" was. They responded simultaneously: Red, pink, blue, red, red and pink, white.

"Was the shirt tucked in or loose?" said Davis. Eager responses suggested that most agreed it was not tucked in well, but three students disagreed, saying it was tucked in all around.

"How would you describe his demeanor? Was he calm or excited, rational or out of control?"

"That's hard to answer," said a student at the back. "He appeared upset, but maybe he had reason if you told him you were going to meet him."

"That wasn't the question," said a girl at the front.

"The question was whether he was upset, not whether he had reason to be upset." A rumble of conversation followed as others commented.

"Okay, okay," said the professor. "How old was he? Students responded in a flurry. Thirty-five; forty; thirty; fifty; twenty-five; thirty.

"Let's move on. What did he say?"

This question was answered by a number of students, all speaking at once: I want to talk with you; are you coming; did you say you're coming; when are you coming out; you're a loser.

"How did I respond?" said Davis. "What did I say?"

The class was involved now. Most of the students responded simultaneously: I'm busy; I have a class; I'll come out after class. Go away, man. A girl at the back, waving her hand, replied loudly: "You said, wait for me in the hall, stupid. I'm done with this bunch, and I'll be right out!" Giggles and general laughter.

"Okay," said Davis, smiling. He looked at the window, back to the class. "Remember what Benjamin said at the outset? What's this all about?" He looked around the classroom, quiet now, attentive.

Thomas, a bespectacled student at the back of the room leaned forward in his chair. "Seems to mean that a bunch of people who are witness to an incident don't always agree on what they saw and heard. In the context of what you said earlier about history and what happened, it means that people who write about the past don't always agree."

"On target," said Davis, pointing at Thomas. "If everyone agreed on what happened during the American Revolution, there would be only one history of the American Revolution. Instead, there are hundreds of histories of the Revolution, and others are published every year.

"Case in point. You're all familiar with a rather important event on January 6 last year." A general muttering of agreement. "Someone tell me in one sentence what happened."

"That's pretty obvious," said Melissa, sitting near the window. Students turned toward her. "A bunch of redneck Trump supporters stormed the capitol, intent on disrupting the government and maybe hanging Mike Pence."

"That's bullshit!" said a student two rows behind her. All turned to see a glowering, red-faced Maurice. "There were some bad apples there, for sure, but most were patriots exercising their constitutional right to protest the tyranny of the Democrats and the theft of the election." This pronouncement was met by guffaws and snickers.

Pam waved her hand back and forth. "I heard on a right-wing news station that it was a bunch of tourists looking for a coffee shop," she said, pulling a face. More snickers and laughter.

"All right, all right," said Davis. "The brilliant observation just now aside, the two other views expressed here made my point more eloquently that I could have done myself. I trust the point is obvious by now: nothing happened in the past unless some historian said it happened. And since historians don't agree on what happened, sometimes we don't know what *really* happened. Each person's bias will determine which version they will accept."

A number of students raised hands, and some began to speak, but they were cut off by Davis who glanced at the clock on the back wall. "We're out of time. That's the end of the story for today. Save it for the next class."

Students stuffed notebooks into packs and cell-phones into pockets, though some still stared at cell-phone screens as they moved toward the hall door, glancing aside at Davis as they went out.

Thomas paused a moment where Davis stood beside his desk. "Sorta makes one wonder why we study history," Thomas said.

"Good point. To be continued," said the professor, clapping Thomas on the shoulder.

———

Davis sat at one of the five small tables on the terrace of Tea With Me, his favorite tea shop. He came here when he wanted to meditate and contemplate. If he wanted to mix with others over coffee or wine, there were other haunts. This place was beyond easy walking distance from the university, and he never invited anyone to come with him or meet him here.

Not since Beth. It was her favorite place as well. He stared at the empty chair, remembering, every time he sat here.

He looked over the railing at the creek about ten feet below. The stream was running full after welcome spring rains. With the diminishing rainfall in succeeding months, the flow of the stream would slow and the depth and width decline, and plants would appear magically on the sloping banks, poppies, alyssum, snapdragon, and lupine.

He loved his solitary terrace seat in all seasons, even in the depth of winter when he could withstand the cold and rain and urging from the staff to come inside out of the weather. He would absolutely refuse if it were snowing.

He sipped from his cup, looked up into the leafy green canopy. Maples and box elders lined the banks of the streambed. The feet of a few of the trees were in the unusually high water, not good if they remained submerged for long.

He waved to a waitress who had stepped outside to wait on a couple who had just arrived and sat at a table near the café door. Davis raised his empty cup, and she nodded.

He looked back to the stream below. *Good response today to the old intruder escapade. Wonder how many semesters I can use that without word getting around? Wish I had used it this semester in the American West class instead of the survey. That's really what's bothering me. Not the Revolution or the Capitol mess. It's the West.*

As long as I've been teaching the West, I'm still conflicted on what really happened. In the American West class, I could find topics for discussion just as convoluted and misunderstood as the Revolution. The Battle of the Little Bighorn. Gad, there are articles and books published ad infinitum, ad nauseam, every year about the Little Bighorn.

Yet, I am interested in the story and look at the new accounts. But I'm becoming saturated. Hasn't everything that can be said about that fiasco been said? My friend, Will Barkley, commented recently about the battle. Will played a mounted soldier in the filming of a documentary about the Little Bighorn. He said it was great fun. I doubt Custer would agree that the day's events were great fun.

This raises another issue. Should historians simply report what they believe happened, or should they make judgments based on evidence? Should they simply tell the story of the Little Bighorn, or should they go further and conclude, based on evidence, that Custer was a vainglorious, ignorant little twit? Gad, how I wish I could have been a fly on the tent wall and listened to the planning. Or materialize and tell Custer what an ass he was.

What about Wounded Knee? I have read scores of accounts of that tragic event and am not convinced that I know what happened. New accounts appear regularly, adding to the narrative and the confusion.

Sand Creek? Originally called a battle, it was later correctly labeled the Sand Creek Massacre. What about the Sioux Wars? Do we really have a clear, unadulterated understanding of the issues and blame for the wars? Should historians spend less time describing events and more time assigning blame, based as much on morality as on planning and execution?

He looked up, startled to see the smiling waitress standing beside the table, tea pot in hand. He pushed his cup across the table. She poured, he thanked her, and she withdrew.

He sipped from the cup. He remembered a question put to him by Christian, his bright, eight-year-old nephew at their last meeting. "Uncle Brett, if you could go to the future or to the past, where would you go?"

Brett remembered pondering. He had talked with Christian on a number of occasions of his fascination about the future and how much he wished he could live to see the day when earthlings almost surely will visit other planets inhabited by intelligent creatures, equivalent to or superior to homo sapiens.

He had also talked with Christian about his concern with the confusion of our understanding of the past. What if he could visit important events in the past, floating around as a vapor or mist, listening and watching? Perhaps he could finally understand what happened and draw conclusions based on this personal experience.

He replied to Christian's question by waffling. "I don't know, buddy. That's a hard question. Can I do both?"

Christian had laughed, grabbed his uncle's hands and squeezed. "I guess so. Can we go get ice cream now?" Davis decided that agreeing to get ice cream was easier than deciding whether to visit the past or the future. He took Christian's hand and headed for the door.

———

Brett stirred the glowing embers with a dry stick and dropped it. The stick burst into flame, burned only a moment and melted into the bed of coals. He looked up into the clear sky, filled with bright stars, glistening, pulsing in the darkness.

This was Beth's favorite campsite, three miles from the end of the county park, accessible only by foot or horseback. No facilities, just bare ground under the scattered oaks that bordered the narrow stream. A thin growth of reeds and low bushes lined the banks. Behind him, the dry pasture grew passable Timothy Grass hay. Across the stream, a few Angus and Hereford cattle were scattered across the good pasture on rolling grassland. At least, they were there before sunset. All he could see now was the leafy canopy above, softly illuminated by the dying fire, and the starry heavens.

He looked up when his horse, hobbled nearby, snorted and stamped. *You all right there, Buddy?* He listened, heard nothing more. Pulling off his boots, he crawled to the sleeping bag behind him, slid in and pulled up the cover.

He stared up into the starry darkness, and his eyes filled. He and Beth camped here occasionally on weekends and always at the end of the spring semester, celebrating, relaxing, winding down. She taught sixth grade for eleven years until she lost the battle with cancer. It was four years since his sweet wife left him alone, and he missed her terribly.

He pulled the cover over his face, wiping his tears on the blanket.

———

He was awakened by distant birdsong. Eyes still closed, he listened a moment to the song, a most welcome invitation to the new day. He opened his eyes and saw clear, blue sky, a few scattered puffs of clouds. Rolling over on his side, he reached for the binocular and pulled the strap over his head. An avid birder, he carried the binocular everywhere.

Pushing the cover down, he sat up and frowned. He shivered, pulled the blanket around his shoulders. *Something's wrong here.* He couldn't see the stream. Dense thickets head high lined what should be the edge of the stream, but he couldn't see the stream. He looked around. His horse was still hobbled close by, still grazing. But beyond the horse, he saw no hay fields, only native grasses, buffalo grass and blue grama, plants common before the land was cleared for cultivation.

He pulled his boots on and stood, looking about, apprehensive. Walking to the streamside thickets, he pushed foliage aside to stand on the bank. He recoiled. The stream, ten feet wide with hardly a perceptible flow when he went to bed, now was twenty feet wide with a stiff current.

Must have been heavy rainfall upcountry during the night. He looked across the stream. *What th' hell!* Instead of shortgrass meadow, a tallgrass prairie with scattered serviceberry and mountain mahogany bushes and low trees covered the land as far as he could see. And not a cow in sight.

Squeezing his eyes shut, he shook his head. *What's going on here?* He opened his eyes, still expecting to see short grass and Herefords. Nothing was changed. He saw only wild prairie.

Closing his eyes, he tried to relax. *Get a hold of yourself. You've been too anxious about Beth, too anxious about what the future holds for you. You've spent too much time musing about the reality of the past, what really happened. You can't know that! It's past, gone. It's distracting you. Let it go. You're... you're hallucinating.*

Opening his eyes, he looked again at the meadow, wanting to see cows, but there were none. He shook his head to clear the cobwebs, then looked again at the meadow. Still empty.

Then he saw movement. Across the field, a line of horsemen rode from behind a low hillock. They appeared to be wearing the same clothing. Uniforms? As more riders came into view, they did indeed appear to be wearing uniforms and riding in formation. Then he saw the flag. A rider near the front of the column carried a flag that hung loosely on its staff. The flag fluttered briefly and opened. It was the American flag.

The riders were too far away to be sure, but the flag didn't look right. Something about the field of stars. There didn't seem to be enough stars. Looking through the binocular, he held steady until another breeze opened the flag. He quickly counted the lines, five, then as the flag fluttered open a longer moment, the horizontal stars in the line, seven. Thirty-five stars.

That's it! This is a reenactment. I wonder what it is, where they are going. But... that doesn't explain the stream or the fields. He squeezed his eyes shut, let the binocular hang, and rubbed his face vigorously with both hands.

He opened his eyes to see two riders coming at a lope. *Now I'll get some answers.*

The two horsemen pulled up on the opposite bank. Davis recognized the uniform of the frontier army. "You okay?" said one of the horsemen. "The lieutenant said you might be in trouble and sent us to find out." The soldiers dismounted and walked their mounts to the stream bank. The horses dipped muzzles into the water.

"No trouble," said Davis. "I'm okay. Are you on a reenactment?"

The soldiers looked at each other. "A what?" said one.

"A reenactment."

"I don't know what a reenactment is, mister, and I

doubt you do. You sure you're okay? You didn't get too much sun, or you been bit by somethin'?"

"Where are you from? Where are you going?" Brett said.

"You sure ask a lot of questions. What're you doin' all by yourself out here, miles from anything?"

"I like to camp in the wild."

"You camp in th' wild too long, and you're gonna meet some of th' wild locals who ain't gonna be too happy with you trespassin' on their lands."

"As a matter of fact," said the other soldier, grinning, "we're on the way to convince some locals to be nice to whites who want to pass through their country."

Brett frowned. His mind raced. "Locals? Indians? What Indians are you out to convince?"

"I don't know. Hostiles."

"They're Cheyennes and Arapahos," the other trooper said. "They've set up at a place called Sand Creek. That's where we're goin'."

Brett recoiled as if struck full in the face. "Your... commander... is?"

"Chivington," said the first soldier, grinning, "Colonel Chivington. He's a real fireball. He hates Indians and knows how to fight 'em. He told us to kill and scalp all of 'em, big and little—"

"Nits make lice," Brett said softly, looking down.

"Yeah, that's what he said! And he said while we're goin' about our business, don't forget that the hostiles have murdered our women and children."

Chivington. Oh, yes, I know about Chivington. Brett had long since formed an opinion of the notorious officer. He had become so incensed on reading the historical record that he remembered this Coloradan well. In spring 1861, Chivington led Colorado volunteers against invading Texas Confederates. He defeated the Texans and destroyed their wagons and supplies. Then at his orders, six hundred horses and mules were killed by bayoneting.

Brett shook his head. *Killing anyone, even enemy soldiers, is barbaric in itself, but domestic animals?* Later, in 1864, Chivington ordered the execution of five members of a gang who were guilty of nothing more than theft.

"You okay?" said one of the soldiers.

Brett looked up. "Where's this Sand Creek?"

"The guide said it was two days' easy ride when I asked him this mornin'." He turned and pointed. "Down that swale. The Colonel said we were going to ride real slow so we can hit the village at first light." The soldier pulled his horse back from the bank. "C'mon, Rog, we gotta git back." He turned to Brett as he mounted. "You better come with us, mister. This country ain't gonna be safe for any white man after we finish the job at Sand Creek."

Brett looked down, shuddered, and shook his head. He felt faint. "I'll be okay."

"You don't look okay. But if that's the way you want it. Hope we don't have to bury you on the way back."

The second soldier snickered as the two riders kicked their horses into a gallop toward the army column that was disappearing behind a low rising.

Brett watched until the soldiers reached the end of the column and were gone. He hurried to his horse and threw on the saddle. As he tightened the cinch, he stopped. A scabbard attached to the saddle held a rifle. *What th' hell!*

He pulled the rifle slowly from the scabbard and examined it. It was a Henry. Jon Harst, his friend and fellow writer, just last week had responded to his question and described the rifle for a manuscript he was working on. Breech-loading and lever action, it was one of the earliest repeating rifles. He frowned. *What a coincidence.* He opened the saddlebags behind the saddle and pulled out a canvas bag of rimfire cartridges.

What else might I find in here? Opening the other saddle bag, he gingerly pulled out a bag he had not placed there. He opened the bag and saw strips of jerky and... biscuits? A half dozen fresh biscuits, as fresh and flaky as if taken from an oven that very morning. He replaced the bag carefully and pulled out his wallet from the saddlebag. The wallet seemed fatter than usual. His eyes opened wide as he took out a stack of fresh, crispy bills. They were United States Notes in different denominations, ones, twos, fives, tens, and a bunch of twenties. He recalled talking about the new currency, first issued in 1862, in an American West lecture a month or so before the end of semester.

He lifted the saddlebag flap, pushed the wallet inside, and stopped. He pulled out a holster holding a pistol. He squinted, his brain churning. He slowly withdrew the pistol. It was an 1860 Colt Army revolver. Harst, a collector as well as an authority on western firearms, only a few months ago had shown him by attachment to an email his recent purchase of an 1860 Colt. *Another coincidence.* Returning the holster to the bag, he untied the coat that he hadn't noticed till now. Nor had he noticed that he was cold. He pulled on the coat and buttoned up.

Brett leaned on his mount. *What in hell is*

happening to me? I'm in Colorado Territory in November 1864.

———

He rode on a dry prairie through buffaloberry and sumac scrub and scattered spruce and pine trees. Pulling up occasionally, he peered through his binocular at the distant army column in the north, visible as a thin dark line on the brown land. Whether riding or stationary, he tried hard to blend with the land in case some sharp-eyed, curious officer caught movement and tried to spot the source with his own binocular. No, it would be a spyglass, a monocular, and would not have the distance or clarity of his twenty-first century binocular.

When the sun was high, he decided he had determined the army's direction and kicked his horse into a lope, soon leaving the plodding army column behind. Moving ahead of them, he worried that he would miss Sand Creek. *If only I could pull out my cellphone and check Google Earth for Sand Creek.* He smiled thinly, shook his head.

He searched his memory for background of the approaching confrontation, what he had covered in lectures. He recalled that Black Kettle and other chiefs had made impassioned peaceful overtures in recent months, principally to Major Wynkoop, commanding officer at Fort Lyon near Denver.

Wynkoop was receptive. He had long advocated making peace with the tribes. On one occasion, he invited leading Cheyenne and Arapaho chiefs, led by Black Kettle, to counsel with Colorado Governor

Evans. The chiefs accepted the invitation, expressed their fervent wish for peace, and agreed to turn over white prisoners they held.

Governor Evans was cool to the delegation's overture. Conflicts, primarily with the Cheyenne, during the spring and summer had been widespread in the region. There was considerable talk at the gathering of the benefits of peace and the universal desire for peace, particularly by the Indian leaders. However, it was well known that Evans had no stomach for negotiation with Indians; he would dictate to them from a position of power and insisted they yield to government authority. He told the chiefs that now that the war between the states was nearing an end, Washington would then employ their armies to settle affairs with the Indians. Colonel Chivington added in an aside to the governor that his rule was to fight Indians until they submit.

Brett recalled reading that Chivington had wanted to lead a force into Texas against the southern rebels, but had been forbidden by Governor Evans who ordered the Colonel to remain in Colorado to deal with the local Indians. Brett wondered whether Chivington was so miffed by Evans's refusal that he would take out his ire on the Indians. Chivington had a reputation.

In spite of the blunt talk from white leaders, the Indian chiefs left the Denver conference believing they had succeeded in laying the groundwork for peace. They were wrong. Hardly had they departed Fort Lyon when Evans commenced work on plans to use the recently formed hundred-day 3rd Colorado Volunteers to move against these same Indians who had come to him, pleading for peace.

Evans was embarrassed by the conference with the

chiefs and was infuriated at Wynkoop for initiating it. Now, he was determined that he would not let an opportunity pass. The 3rd Colorado Volunteers had been formed to kill Indians, and by damn, they would kill Indians! If they did not, it would reflect badly on him since the unit had been formed at his instigation.

———

Brett rode alternately at a lope and a walk. Stopping at a narrow stream, he watered his mount and let him graze a few minutes. Then he was off again, stopping occasionally to scan the landscape to the north for any sign of the army column.

At dusk, he made camp at the foot of the south side of a hillock, hoping the army did not send out advance scouting patrols. He was shivering from the November cold before he finished hobbling his horse. Shielded by the hillock, he would chance a fire. Or would he? Going to his horse, he rummaged around in a saddlebag. He pulled out the food sack and, with a sigh of relief, a small box of matches.

He felt around the bottom of the bag. *Anything else in here?* He pulled out three matchbooks, labeled *Tea With Me*. He smiled, remembering picking up the matchbooks on his last visit to the tearoom, then later pushing them into the saddlebags to use when camping.

He collected dry sticks and soon had a low fire built. *What's for supper?* He pulled out some jerky. The biscuits were finished at noon. He wondered how long he could survive on jerky. No problem, as he expected to arrive at Sand Creek the next day.

No problem? How will I be received? What will I

say to them? "You are about to be slaughtered by the United States Army?" What, in fact, can I do?

I am here, about to arrive at the Sand Creek encampment of Cheyenne and Arapaho people. Scores of histories of this affair have been written, beginning just after it happened into the twenty-first century. It's done. It's written. Can I change anything?

Wait. Historians have written what they believe happened. But did they cover everything? Every single incident in that affair? Did something happen that they did not cover, something of which they weren't even aware?

After a skimpy supper of jerky and water, he unrolled his blankets, removed his boots, and lay down, staring up into the void. He finally slept, fitfully, napping, tossing and turning, agonizing.

———

Brett rode in a parched landscape, mostly flat or gently rolling sand hills, covered with dry grasses and occasional stunted mesquites. There was no sign of life in any direction, two-legged or four-legged. He reined up often, searched the land to the north with his binocular, and saw nothing but the land, sandhills with a scattering of mesquite trees. Squinting at the sun, he judged that it must be mid-afternoon.

What led me to think I could find Sand Creek? I'm no pathfinder. I could have missed it by fifty miles.

He rode over the top of a low rising and pulled up. There it was. He sat his horse, looking down on a sizable village of lodges, he guessed more than a hundred, most on a bottom below a low bluff along the shallow ice-crusted creek, some on the flat above the bluff. A few wispy smoke spirals rose from cooking fires. Scattered cottonwoods and willows, their branches bare, grew in the creek bottom and on the banks. Below a bend, eight lodges lined the bank. *Those would be the small contingent of Arapahos.* North of the camp, a large herd of at least five hundred horses grazed in a meadow, the icy grass glistening in the afternoon sun.

Some boys at the herd stood like statues, staring at Brett.

He rode slowly down the rising. Two of the boys at the herd ran toward the lodges, shouting and waving their arms, pointing at Brett. People in the village left chores and emerged from lodges, all looking at the solitary stranger approaching.

Brett held up an arm in greeting, then stretched his arms to each side to show he had no weapons. He reined up at a gathering of perhaps two dozen people. Scores of others, standing beside lodges, watched. As Brett dismounted, a man motioned to a boy to take his reins.

"Does anyone speak English?" said Brett.

A few people shook heads; others simply stared. A man who stood before the other people turned and said something to the youth beside him. The boy ran toward the interior of the village.

While they waited, Brett pondered. He smiled, looked around. *They suspect nothing. In these perilous times, don't they have scouts out to watch for strangers approaching the village? I saw no one until I topped the rising back there and saw the village. Do they feel that secure?*

Brett smiled at the entourage before him, looked

toward the village, the stream, and the countryside. He fidgeted. Shadows of lodges and trees cast by the late afternoon sun lengthened. His mind raced. *Where is the army now? Are they still marching, or have they arrived just over the horizon and are now camped, preparing for tomorrow's attack?*

He recalled reading about the aftermath of the Denver meeting with Governor Evans. Major Wynkoop returned to Fort Lyon and invited the Cheyenne and Arapahoe to camp close to the fort where they would be safe. As an expression of their total reliance on Wynkoop and the army, the chiefs offered to assist the soldiers in fighting the Kiowas and Comanches.

Evans was infuriated with Wynkoop's plan. He arranged the replacement of Wynkoop with Major Scott Anthony who Evans thought more receptive to authority. In fact, Anthony agreed to continue Wynkoop's policy to permit the Indians to camp near the Fort.

Hardly had Wynkoop departed Fort Lyon on November 26 than Anthony had second thoughts, fearing he might have exceeded his authority. He could not have forgotten how Governor Evans felt about the Indians. So he withdrew his protection of the Indians and ordered them to move from the vicinity of Fort Lyon. At the same time, he promised the chiefs that no war would be waged against them.

The Indians did not seem to be alarmed at the change. They did not complain, feeling quite safe. With the good wishes of Major Anthony, who gave Black Kettle a gift at the parting, the Cheyenne broke camp, moved forty miles away, and set up their village at a site on Sand Creek.

Brett shook his head, stared at the village of lodges where people had returned to chores and conversation. *This is bizarre. What am I doing here? Where is there a mention of Brett Davis in any of the histories of Sand Creek? I am here as much as Black Kettle is here. The histories mention Black Kettle repeatedly. Why not Brett Davis?*

"Who are you? What do you want?"

He jumped, startled. He saw the woman who had walked up unnoticed. He was speechless. She was young, perhaps twenty years old, pretty, wearing a fringed buckskin dress. Her long hair waved gently in the light breeze. He was dumbstruck. *She's stunning!*

She glared at him. "Who are you? What you want?"

He blinked. "I am a friend. I have to tell you; you are in danger. The army is coming. They are probably camped nearby right now. They will attack your village tomorrow morning."

She recoiled, looked at the elders who stood beside her. She spoke rapidly to the man who had summoned her. He frowned, looked at Brett. He shook his head, turned and spoke to a man behind him. The man nodded and set out toward the village, running, walking, running. He disappeared beyond a line of lodges.

She faced Brett. "We wait," she said.

Minutes passed. No one moved, no one came.

Brett looked at the sun, now approaching the horizon. He felt dizzy, wavered. The woman caught his arm, said something rapidly to a boy. Taking Brett's arm, she walked him a few steps aside and helped him sit. She sat beside him. A moment passed, and the boy brought a gourd of water and gave it to her. She passed it to him. He took the gourd, nodded his thanks, and drank.

He studied her profile as she stared at the setting sun. Just as he was about to speak, he saw a half dozen men coming. The woman stood quickly, then reached down to help him stand.

Oh my god! It's Black Kettle. The man at the front of the group held his blankets loosely as he approached. Brett had seen many pictures of the Cheyenne chief and easily recognized him. He was about sixty years old, a wise, respected leader who had long sought peace fervently for his people. Brett decided instantly that he had never seen anyone so calm and commanding. He had to restrain himself from bowing. The chief stopped before him and the woman.

"Black Kettle," said Brett.

The chief turned to the woman, questioning. She shook her head. Black Kettle and the woman stared at Brett, then spoke softly to each other in their language. As they talked, she pointed to the east, nodding as he questioned her, glancing occasionally at Brett.

Brett marveled that he was standing before Black Kettle, but he stared at the woman instead. She noticed his stare, turned her back to him, still talking to Black Kettle.

The throng standing behind Black Kettle parted to permit a striding man to come to Black Kettle's side. The woman spoke to him rapidly as he listened, nodding.

The man turned to Brett. "I am Niwot. I speak for Black Kettle." He gestured toward the woman. "Winona say you say army come to attack our village.

This cannot be true. Governor Evans say the army will protect us. He sent us to camp at Fort Lyon so army can protect us. Then Major Anthony said we should move to Sand Creek, and the army would protect us here. We are safe here."

"Niwot, Black Kettle," said Brett, "everything has changed. There are new officers in charge, and they listen to Governor Evans who has changed his mind. He is not a friend of the Indian people; he is an enemy. You must believe me."

Niwot spoke rapidly to Black Kettle. They faced Brett, frowning. "How do you know this?" said Niwot. "Are you from the fort? Who are you? Where do you come from? Why should we believe you and not Governor Evans?"

Brett grimaced. *What can I say to convince them?* "Do you know Colonel Chivington?"

Niwot frowned. He turned to Black Kettle, spoke rapidly, turned back to Brett. "I know Chivington. He is bad man. How do you know him?"

"Colonel Chivington commands the army that comes to attack you."

Niwot translated for Black Kettle who answered slowly, his face placid. Niwot turned back to Brett. "We do not believe you. How you know this?"

A man standing behind Black Kettle stepped up between the chief and Niwot. He spoke to Black Kettle in Cheyenne. Niwot turned to the man, frowning at the interruption.

Black Kettle looked down, pursed his lips. He replied slowly, looking aside at Niwot. The man spoke again to Black Kettle, raising his voice, agitated. Other warriors nearby whispered among themselves, gesturing toward the speaker.

Black Kettle, his face blank, raised a hand, signaling an end to the conversation. He put a hand on the speaker's shoulder. The man, frowning, stepped back into the group behind Black Kettle. He grimaced, looked aside.

Black Kettle nodded to Niwot who turned to Brett. "How do you know these things?"

"I was camped on the prairie. Two soldiers from the army came to my camp and told me about the army's plan to attack your camp tomorrow at first light. They said Chivington leads the force. Chivington has said repeatedly that he wants to kill Indians."

Niwot and Black Kettle talked softly. The woman stood nearby, listening.

Niwot and Black Kettle turned to Brett. "We will talk about what you say." He gestured toward the woman. "Winona will find place for you." Niwot and Black Kettle walked toward the camp. The boy who held Brett's reins handed them to him and ran to join the others who wandered toward the camp, chatting and gesturing, some looking back at Brett.

Winona stayed, watching Brett who drooped, spent. "Do you want stay in village tonight?" she said. "Or do you want to leave before soldiers come?" She almost smiled, looked aside.

"No one believes me. I don't know what I want to do." He looked up at her. "Do you believe me?"

She cocked her head. "I am woman. I listen to the wise men who lead our people, and I follow them."

"They are not wise at the moment." He looked at the horizon where the memory of the sun colored the lacy cloud layers many shades of red, pink and orange.

"You hungry?" she said.

He looked up, breathed deeply, exhaled. "I am indeed hungry."

She walked toward the village, looked back at him. He followed, leading his horse.

"Where is Black Kettle's lodge?" he said. She pointed at a lodge on the embankment above the stream. He wanted to see the large American flag given to him in Washington by President Lincoln, but remembered from his readings that the flag, with a white flag on the same lodgepole staff, was not raised until after the firing began.

Instinctively, he now hoped he would not see the flag tonight or tomorrow. *But the histories say he raised the flag! Can anything change because I am here?*

CHAPTER 2

Winona and Brett sat beside a low fire in front of a lodge. They pulled pieces of meat from the carcass of a rabbit that lay on a stone beside the fire.

Winona wrinkled her nose. "I no like rabbit," she said.

He licked his fingers, pulled off another sliver. "I hope the hunters are successful. Most of your men are hunting today."

She looked sharply at him. "You scare me. How you know these things? Are you shaman or someone who knows what he no see?"

He said nothing, continued eating. Finally: "The man who stood behind Black Kettle and spoke to him did not seem to agree with Black Kettle, like he did not agree the village was safe."

She frowned. "He know more about white man's ways than most in village, even Black Kettle, I think. His father is white, and he went to white man's schools far away. His name is—"

"George Bent."

Her eyes opened wide. "Stop it! How you know him? I will think you a bad spirit if you keep doing this!"

How can I tell her? Yes, I know you, George Bent, or about you. Son of William Bent, who built and operated Bent's Fort, a trading station on the Santa Fe Trail, and his wife, the Cheyenne Owl Woman, you are an intriguing historical figure. Educated in white schools on the Mississippi, forever trying to encourage peace with whites while trying at the same time to protect your Indian people. We saw you here at Sand Creek and heard you try to make sense of what you knew was coming, but the others were not as knowing as you. I don't understand Cheyenne, but it was obvious what you were saying.

He looked at Winona, resisted the temptation to smile. He pulled a piece of meat from the bone, jerked away quickly, shaking his hand. "Ouch. That's hot." He touched the rabbit again lightly, pulled off a sliver of meat.

"Where did you learn English?" he said. "You speak well."

She looked grimly at him, then softened and looked aside. "I don't talk about it much. It was sad, happy time. My father and mother were killed in battle with whites. The whites took me with them. I was ten or twelve. I lived with this white man and his wife, a white woman, five years. The man treated me like slave. His wife treated me like a person. She good woman. She help me learn English and teach me to read." She looked down, smiled a shy smile. "I can write a little, not much. The man did not like this. He said it would give me ideas. He always mean to me, and he got more mean every day. His wife tried protect me from him, but he told her the Indian was his business.

"One time he tried do bad things to me on my bed. She come in and pull him off me. He very angry and hit her hard. That was enough for her. He always bad to her, but he never hit her. She told me he would not do that again. She said be ready to leave during night when he sleeping. She would give him lots of whiskey at dinner so he not wake up.

"After dark, when he sleeping, she come to kitchen where my bed was, and we go out back door. She had her horse ready, and she give me his horse. Oh, he was going be mad!

"We ride till the sun was high when we saw some Indians on trail. The woman scared sick, but I said it was okay. I recognize they are Cheyenne by their clothes. We lucky. I yell to them, and we ride to them. I tell them everything. They laugh so hard, they almost fall off horses.

"We ride together on trail toward Denver. That's where she say she want to go. The Cheyenne finally say they return to their village and ask me if I want ride with them. She thank me and ride away. I wish her luck. I still wonder if she reach Denver. She was good to me. Her name was Sarah." She stared at the glowing embers. "She call me 'Winnie'. She say it was name of her friend who was killed in fight when whites kill my mother and father."

She looked up from the fire. "Are you good white man? I haven't known many good white people. I don't know your name."

He smiled thinly. "Brett. Am I a good white man? I

try to be good, but that's up to others to decide whether I'm good or bad. I think your people here think I'm bad. Or crazy."

They looked at each other a long moment. She stared down into the embers. "I want believe you. You seem good man, and you seem to believe what you say is true. But it different from all we have been told, all we understand. We feel safe. But you say we not safe. You say we are in danger."

They were quiet, staring into the low flames. He studied her profile, her smooth, brown cheeks, small nose, soft lips. Loose strands of black hair fell over her temples. He resisted a strong impulse to touch her.

"What does your name mean?" he said.

She looked aside at him. "It mean I know lot of things. Uh, smart, intelligent, George Bent say."

"I understand. I think George Bent is right." He picked up some dry sticks from the pile behind him, dropped them on the fire. "I'm going to call you 'Winnie'. Is that all right?" She smiled, nodded.

"Do you speak Arapahoe as well as Cheyenne?" he said.

"Yes, I have many Arapahoe friends when I was small and when I returned from living with the whites." She turned to him. "Do you speak other languages than English?"

He smiled. "No. Most of my people speak only one language. We are ignorant on languages."

She looked back to the fire. "I speak Sioux. Not good, but I can speak with Sioux people, and they understand."

"I'm surprised. Where did you learn Sioux?"

"Old Sioux man and old Sioux woman live with

same whites that I lived with. They were in a Sioux hunting camp when white men attack them. The whites said that the Sioux had been carrying off their cows and horses. The whites killed twelve men and women and took four people prisoners. The white man I live with took a man and a woman. He said he would put them to work for him.

"When I go to live with white man and woman, the Sioux had been with them four or five years. I ask them why they not run away. The man said he know the whites going take over the country, and he said he was tired of all the fighting. He said he and his woman not worked too hard, and they had enough to eat. He said they were satisfied and would stay.

"I work a lot with Sioux woman, and I liked her. Her name was Tashina. She was smart woman, but she hardly ever say anything to the whites or her husband. I learn Sioux language from Tashina."

"Why didn't you run away?"

"I was young. I was afraid. I did try one time run away. He caught me and beat me. I thought he would kill me."

Winona had been looking into the low flames as she spoke. Now she was quiet and still looked down into the fire that had burned down to embers. Brett waited a moment, then looked through the tent opening to the darkness outside. Turning back to her, he took her hand. She started to pull away but let him hold it.

"Winnie, will you do this for me? Will you let me saddle both our horses and hobble them near your lodge? Pack some food and have it ready. Sleep in your clothes. If trouble comes in the morning, we'll ride away. If there is no trouble, we'll go for an early ride.

We'll listen to the birds singing and watch for the hunters coming back."

She frowned, looked down. "Yes, I do this." She stood, looked around. "This my lodge. It is yours tonight. I will sleep in next lodge. It belong two brothers who are hunting. I watch their lodge when they away." She went to the entrance and threw back the flap, looked back. "I will make sack of food while you saddle the horses and hobble them. We will ride from village tomorrow, and I will show you pretty sunrise."

He hobbled the horses on a patch of grass near his lodge. Going back inside, he brought out blankets and tied them behind the saddles. They would sleep on the prairie tomorrow night.

———

Boom! He sat bolt upright. Then again, Boom! Boom! He threw the covers off, frantically pulled on his boots, and stood. He bent to pick up the gun belt and strapped it on.

"What is that?" shouted Winona.

He jerked around to see her silhouette in the tent entrance, holding the tent flap open. He saw over her shoulder that it was first light.

He rushed to her. "Cannon. The army is attacking." Then pop, pop, pop of rifle fire. The shots came from the east across the creek. "Go to your lodge and get the food. Hurry! I'll get the horses."

She ran to her lodge while he removed the hobbles from the horses and led them to her lodge. She came out, handed him a small bag, and took her reins. He stuffed the bag in his saddlebag and mounted. She held her reins, frozen, looking toward the creek where a line of soldiers waded in the shallow water.

"Mount!" he said softly, urgently. The trance broke, and she pulled up on her horse. He kicked his horse into a gallop, and she followed. They rode westward along the embankment, past lodges where people stood about, confused, looking around. A few men and boys came from lodges, carrying rifles and bows. They ran toward the edge of the village, toward the army riflemen and cannon.

Galloping along the embankment, Brett saw Black Kettle and Niwot frantically raising a lodgepole holding the American flag and a white flag below while Black Kettle's wife watched. Brett shook his head and kicked his horse, shouting to Winona to ride faster. He knew that Black Kettle would be forcefully carried off the field by his warriors. His wife would be shot eight times and survive.

Brett straightened when he saw an Indian standing rigid in the creek bed, his arms folded across his chest. Brett's eyes misted. He had told the story of White Antelope often in his American West classes. White Antelope had run from the village toward the troops, empty hands held high, a peace sign, yelling at the troops not to fire. Now he stood quietly, awaiting death. His heroic action was lost on the troops. They shot him dead where he stood.

Brett shook his head vigorously and drummed his horse's belly with his heels. He looked ahead with alarm to see the head and shoulders of a trooper at the front of a line of soldiers struggling up a steep cut in the embankment.

Too late to stop. He drew his pistol. The soldier in

the lead saw Brett and Winona coming. He fumbled with his rifle and brought it up clumsily, but too late. Brett was almost on him when he fired, hitting the trooper in the shoulder, spinning him around and into the soldiers behind him. Some fell aside as others tumbled backwards to the creek bed.

He kicked his horse and yelled at Winona, "Ride! Ride! Ride!" The sounds of shots fired at them by the soldiers on the embankment faded as they galloped from the village.

———

Brett and Winona sat beside a low fire. They ate jerky from a bag on the ground between them. Both stared into the flames. They had ridden for hours and had hardly spoken since stopping at the sheltered place at the base of a low rising.

She looked at her clasped hands in her lap, then turned to him. "Now you must tell me."

How do I do this?

"You know everything about the army," she said. "How do you know this? Are you from army?"

He inhaled deeply. "Winona. Winnie. I will tell you. You will think me mad." He looked aside. *Maybe I am mad.*

"Winnie. I am not from the army. I come from far away. Far away in time. This year, today, here in Colorado Territory, the year is 1864. I come from the year 2022, over one hundred fifty years in the future."

She recoiled, frowning, looked abruptly at him. She pursed her lips. "I don't understand."

He inhaled deeply. "I don't either." He leaned

forwarded, looked into the low flames. "I don't know how this happened. I was camping at a place in my time where my wife and I had camped often before she died. I went to bed and woke up in your time in a strange place. I talked with some soldiers and found that I was near Sand Creek.

"I knew what happened at Sand Creek. I had read about what happened. In books, it is called the Sand Creek Massacre. I knew what happened here before I arrived. I knew about George Bent because I have read about him. I have seen pictures of him in books.

"I know about Black Kettle. He is very famous in history. I tried to tell him and the others about the army, and I understand why they did not believe me. If I told them what I am telling you now, they would think me mad. Some would call me an evil shaman and would want to kill me." He turned to her. "Do you believe me?"

She stared at him, her face blank. She looked at her hands in her lap, then faced him. "I believe... this is what you believe." She looked up at the sun, now high in the cloudless blue sky. A cold breeze picked up, and she shuddered. "What we do now?"

He studied the flames. "We could keep riding, but you would never accept what you cannot know. We will return to the village. It's safe now."

"How can you..."

He scraped up a double handful of soil and sprinkled it on the fire. Standing, he offered her his hand. She took the hand and stood, walked behind him to the hobbled horses. She stood silently, watching him, her face blank. He removed the hobbles and stowed them in his saddle bags.

They mounted and kicked their horses into a lope eastward.

———

Brett and Winona rode into the village when the sun hung low above the western horizon. They rode into chaos and carnage. Smoke rose from fires throughout the village. Bodies still lay strewn about among smoldering lodges and on the edge of the village. Most were women, and many were children. A great number were scalped. One woman was split open from chin to waist, and her unborn child lay lifeless beside her. Some women had gaping holes in their chests, their breasts having been cut off. Brett remembered an account of the massacre that told of a soldier bragging that he was going to make a tobacco pouch of his breast trophies.

It was the women who suffered most in the attack since most of the men were away hunting. Brett had been horrified when he read about the massacre in the histories. Now he saw the results with his own eyes. Women had thrown up their hands to show they had no weapons. They were shot and killed. When soldiers discovered five women hiding on a creek bank, the women stood and exposed their breasts to show they were not warriors, and the soldiers shot them down. Thirty or forty women had cowered in a hole in a sand embankment. When they saw the soldiers coming, they sent out a little girl of six years carrying a white flag on a stick. The soldiers shot her dead.

Winona saw the carnage, paralyzed, shuddering. She leaned against Brett. Soldiers who saw them paused, pondered, rode by. Brett stared at them, his hand resting on his pistol grip. He had a hard time not drawing his Colt and firing. He was restrained only by the sure knowledge that both he and Winona would be killed without hesitation.

Brett saw a solitary soldier, an officer, standing on the edge of the village, head hanging. Brett stared at him, frowning. The soldier rubbed his face with both hands, looked around vacantly. Brett walked to him, holding Winona's hand. The officer looked at them, eyes red and moist.

"Captain Soule, I think," said Brett.

The soldier turned slowly to Brett. "Yes. Do I know you?"

"I understand you did not order your men to fire today."

Soule frowned at him, looked vacantly toward the village. "That's true. I wanted no part of it. We're supposed to be protecting them, not killing them. That didn't prevent my men from firing. They got the killing fever and wanted to be a part of it. They fired, and I couldn't stop them. They are more Chivington's men than mine." He squinted, looked at Brett. "Do I know you?"

"No, but I know about you. You're a good man. Not many of those on the field today." Soule raised a hand and started to speak, but Brett strode away, pulling Winona along. *Better not get involved at this moment in history. Soule was indeed a good man. Shortly he will return to Denver where he will be shot dead in the street.*

Winona stopped. "How did you know him? Captain Soule? Have you met him before?"

Brett looked around, took her hand and walked to a mesquite tree. He stopped, took both her hands, looked her full in the face, spoke slowly. "Winnie. I have never met him. I have never seen him before today. I read about Soule in a book published over one hundred years after the massacre. The book included pictures of him. Do you begin to understand my situation? My predicament?"

Her face clouded, and she slumped. Brett put his arms around her shoulders and drew her to him, holding her.

After a long moment, she pulled back, and he released her. "I scared," she said. "I so confused."

He held her hands. "Can you accept that I know what is going to happen before it happens? Can you accept that?"

"Yes, I think so."

"Good. Then listen. The killing in this village has finished for now, but it is not a safe place to be. The warriors are returning from their hunt, and they will be angry. They will want revenge. This will be true in the entire region.

"Before, it was only the young men who wanted to make a name for themselves that attacked wagon trains and isolated farms and ranches. That wasn't new. That's what young warriors have been doing for hundreds of years. But most Cheyenne and Arapaho people wanted peace and got along well for the most part with whites.

"There was a time when it appeared that there might be a lasting peace here. The Cheyenne and Arapahoe in a treaty in 1861, just three years ago, agreed to give up all their lands in exchange for a reservation in southeastern Colorado Territory, mostly barren country with no game, but under the treaty, the government was going to help them change their way of life, from people who lived free, following the buffalo and moving wherever they wished. The government was going to help them become farmers. The government was going to give them farm equipment and fencing, and they would send farmers and mechanics to teach them how to use the new equipment. They were going to build them a sawmill, shops, and houses. Each Indian was to own forty acres of land.

"Do you see what was happening? Government was going to change the Arapaho and Cheyenne people into white people, and the Cheyenne and Arapaho chiefs agreed. They signed the treaty in February 1861.

"This doesn't mean there was always peace. Fighting had been part of their way of life, and there continued to be incidents. At the invitation of government, a party of chiefs visited Washington in 1863. They talked with President Lincoln. This seemed to reassure the chiefs, but it wasn't Lincoln the chiefs had to contend with back on the plains. It was the local authorities.

"An army officer in Colorado during this time of increasing conflict said that government must decide what was the best way of dealing with Indians—feed them or let them starve. He said that the latter, letting them starve, might be the easiest way to be rid of them.

"Cheyenne and Arapaho sometimes warred against other tribes, as they always had, but of all the tribes, they were most friendly toward whites. Once when they had fought the Utes, a band of Cheyenne and Arapaho even paraded down Denver streets, holding up five fresh Ute scalps. They wouldn't have done that in Denver if they feared and hated white people.

"Most whites had a hard time believing Indians could be peaceful. As late as last summer, June I think, a rumor that hostile Indians were coming to Denver caused panic, and people got ready, sending women and children to safe places and stocking up on ammunition. No Indians showed up, but it shows how whites feared Indians.

"That's when Governor Evans decided to separate the good Indians from the bad, sending the peaceful Indians to Fort Lyon where they would be safe and supervised, where the agent would give them provisions.

"Sand Creek changed everything. Now even the Indians who wanted peace with the whites are outraged and will want revenge for this betrayal. Other tribes are going to rise as well. What happened here at Sand Creek convinced Indians everywhere they can't trust whites. The Sioux are going to ride with the Cheyenne on northern trails. Comanches and Kiowas will attack whites in Texas. These things will happen. I have read books that say this will happen."

"What should we do?"

"Hey! You!" Brett and Winona turned to see two mounted soldiers rein up behind them. "What are you doing here? You're not with the army."

Brett stammered. "Uh, I'm here... on official business."

The lieutenant glared at Winona, back to Brett. "What do you mean, official business? What office, what agency?"

Brett opened his mouth to reply, but nothing came out. *What do I say to this cretin?* "I'm here to—"

"Lieutenant!" Everyone jerked around to see a

soldier reining up hard to a sliding stop, showering all with dust. "The Colonel needs to talk to you! Quick!"

The lieutenant scowled at Brett. "You stay where I can find you!" He and the other soldier kicked their horses into a gallop after the messenger who had already set off.

They watched the riders a moment. Brett exhaled. He didn't realize that he had been holding his breath. *I was lucky. I've got to be ready for this sort of situation. From now on, I must know who I am at any moment.*

"What should we do?" she said again, softly.

He pondered. "We can't say here. We need to find a safe place." He held her hands. "You said, 'what should *we* do?' Come with me. Will you come with me?"

She ducked her head. "Yes. I have no one."

"You have me." He looked around. "I don't think most of the soldiers will bother me. They don't know what to make of me. The lieutenant just now is another matter. The army will leave soon, but we need to go before any of them decide to come looking for me." He took her arm. "Let's go to your lodge. I don't think anyone will search for me during the night. They have too much on their minds. Pack whatever food we can carry. I'll take care of the horses. I'm going to find a loose horse to pack some things. We need to leave tomorrow before daylight."

———

Brett woke at a soft rustling beside his bed. He saw nothing in the darkness and slowly reached for the pistol at his head. Winona touched his hand. He saw her dim outline kneeling beside his bed.

He raised on an elbow. "Are you okay?"

"I am cold. I scared."

He lifted the blanket. She crept inside and lay beside him, shivering. Replacing the cover, he put his arms around her, pulled her to him, their bodies entwined, and she was still.

She snuggled against his chest. "I call you 'Brett'."

———

Brett pushed the tent flap aside and looked out. Moonlight softly illuminated the embankment and creek bed beyond. Bare tree limbs cast black striped shadows over the lodge and the three horses hobbled nearby. He listened a full minute and heard nothing but the mournful howl of a distant wolf. He looked back inside, and Winona touched his arm.

He studied her face, softly outlined by moonlight, her dark eyes focused on his, her hair a halo of loose strands. He took her face in his hands and softly kissed her lips. She put a hand to his cheek. He took the hand in his and turned to look outside.

They crept from the tent, Brett carrying a filled hide bag and Winona two saddle blankets. Brett's horse snuffled at his approach. He touched the horse's muzzle, and the horse shook its head. Tying the bag on the packhorse, he hurried to the lodge and brought out two saddles. He bridled and saddled the horses while Winona worked on the hobbles.

He stuffed the hobbles into his saddlebag and took the reins of the packhorse from Winona. They mounted, touched their horses' bellies lightly with their heels, and rode westward at a walk along the embankment. Moonlight made shadows of lodges and the few horses hobbled or tied to stakes.

Both started at the sound of a child crying. They searched the darkness and saw no one.

Winona reined her horse against Brett. She leaned toward him, whispered, "She may be alone. Her mother maybe killed."

"We can't stop," he whispered, "someone will hear her." They rode on, and the crying continued, diminishing gradually as they rode out of hearing. Finally, there was no sound but the soft padding of horses' hooves.

Brett frowned, eyes clenched and head hanging. *In this surreal experience, does everything that happens have meaning beyond what we see? Is the child the Indian people who cry out for something, someone to help them, to save them? If that is true, then my decision not to go to her is a fulfillment of history. If that is true, would anything have changed if we had gone to her?*

He shook his head vigorously. *Stop it! Just stop it! You'll go insane if you go on like this.*

———

The sun ball hung just above the eastern horizon, lightly tinting layers of wispy horizontal clouds. A soft vapor rose from the ice-encrusted grasses. Brett and Winona rode on a lightly rutted road in a rolling prairie. He guessed this was a wagon road that led toward Denver. *Do we want to go to Denver?*

His musing was interrupted by the appearance of a dozen or so horsemen ahead. They rode from the meadow onto the road and turned toward Brett and

Winona. Brett exhaled. They were cowboys, not soldiers.

"What we do?" she said, softly.

"Keep riding. Too late to run now."

The riders ahead pulled up and waited. Brett and Winona reined up before them.

"Mornin', boys," said Brett.

"Who are you, where you headed? What's your business?" said a rider at the front of the group.

Brett studied the riders. They appeared to be anything but bad men out to do harm, rather average fellows who would rather be doing what they did for a living than riding out to do somebody else's business.

"Well," said Brett, "we're heading toward Denver if you'll confirm that we're on the right road."

"This is the road. What's your business?"

Brett noticed that the only person in the group looking at him was the speaker. The others stared at Winona, some grinning and whispering to each other.

"I'm, uh, with the railroad survey. We have a survey team looking at the prospect for a southern route across Texas and New Mexico to California."

The rider frowned, looked at his pardners. "Never heard about that. There ain't no talk about railroads around here. Anybody heard about railroads here-abouts?" The others shook heads, still staring at Winona.

"Really? There are railroad survey teams down in the Southwest and another one looking for a route from the Mississippi to Cheyenne. What I'm about to do is meet with a few surveyors and town leaders in Denver to talk about a spur from Denver to Cheyenne to tie in with that line."

The spokesman frowned. "I ain't never heard any of this talk, and I go to Denver ever now and then."

Brett smiled. "Maybe you don't talk with the right people. What's your bunch up to? I don't s'pose you're out ridin' for pleasure."

"No, we ain't. We're looking for a bunch of young bucks that stole a dozen horses from a ranch a few miles east of here. Indians around here been pretty peaceful, but the young 'uns seem always to be a problem." He gestured toward Winona. "Who's she? She speak English?"

"She's my interpreter. Yes, she speaks better English than most cowboys, and three Indian languages as well." Riders behind the speaker snickered.

The man stared at Winona, his face blank. "I 'spect she's useful in more ways than just interpretin'." More grins and snickers from the cowboys.

Brett said nothing, simply glared at the speaker. He thought of a dozen responses, including shooting him out of his saddle, but decided he had best tiptoe lightly. He marveled that he even generated the thought. *What's happening to me?*

The man studied Brett, then Winona, back to Brett. He looked ahead. "I 'spect we'd best be on our way. I don't s'pose you saw any Indians on this trail."

"Nope. Only thing wild we've seen for days are coyotes and rabbits." He reined off the road so the cowboys could pass. Winona followed, ignoring the grins and hungry stares. "Good luck with the hunt," Brett said.

The leader of the bunch moved off, followed by the others. "Good luck with the railroad," he threw over his shoulder. "Sure could use it to move cattle and soldiers."

The cowboys kicked their horses into a lope down the road. Brett looked at Winona, exhaled heavily. "They've not heard about Sand Creek. They would have had lots more questions if they had." They watched the group until they disappeared down a dip in the road.

Winona frowned. "Why we go to Denver?"

He smiled. "I thought nothing could surprise me during this strange episode in my life, then you say: 'Why we go to Denver?'"

"I don't understand."

"Because I was just about to say: 'Why are we going to Denver?'"

"Well?"

"Well, we are not going to Denver. Somebody is riding to Denver right now on a fast horse to tell Governor Evans what happened at Sand Creek. Chivington and the hundred-day volunteers will arrive in Denver shortly where they will be welcomed as heroes on a job well done. I have read about this in my time, but I forgot. Somebody in that lot likely will tell about this strange fellow who was in camp, claiming to be on official business. And there's likely to be someone who saw us in Sand Creek who would go ballistic if he saw us in Denver."

She pursed her lips. "What is bull...iss...tick?"

He smiled, a hint of a smile. "Never mind. Later. Question now is, where can we go?"

They sat, silent, staring at the country, reflecting, pondering.

"We go to Bent's Fort," Winona said.

CHAPTER 3

Brett and Winona sat at a low campfire. Their horses were hobbled near the narrow stream behind the camp. He tossed into the coals the last bones of the rabbit they had roasted earlier. He wiped his hands on the grass.

"That was good," he said. She looked at him, frowned. "Yeah, I know. You don't like rabbit." He leaned toward her, put a hand to her cheek and kissed her lips. She smiled thinly, looked into the embers. He stirred the coals with a stick, tossed it into the pit, and it immediately caught fire and flamed briefly.

He was surprised at first when Winona said they should go to Bent's Fort. He had always been fascinated with the fort, though he had spent little time on it in his lectures. Now he was delighted that he was going to visit it.

Constructed in 1833 as a trading post for Indians and trappers, it became an important gathering point for traders, travelers, and Indians. In the 1840s, it became a way station for wagon trains that traveled between Missouri and Santa Fé. Winona would know about the fort, though she said she had never been there. Cheyenne and Arapahoe early on visited the fort regularly, trading buffalo robes for white man's goods, chiefly guns, ammunition, blankets, and clothing.

This is a good idea. We'll have a safe place, out of sight, time to decide what's next for us.

———

They sat at a small campfire of red and golden flames, looking up into the deep blue sky, filled with a mass of sparkling stars. A soft, cold breeze fanned the flames, sending sparks flying.

"I wish it was always this peaceful," Brett said.

She did not respond, still staring up into the void. After a long moment, she turned to him. "Why do white people hate Indian people so much?"

He pondered, paused a long moment. *How do I answer this?* He took her hand, looked into her eyes.

"It's more complicated than it appears, but I'll try. White people have always believed that they are better than people with colored skin, and they don't treat these people fairly. Not all whites believe this, but most believe it.

"Then when white people decided to move west, they came up against Indian people who had lived on the land for centuries and believed the land was theirs to use as they wished. It was their land. Indian people had always lived a free life, following the seasons and the buffalo.

"Whites would not accept that Indians had any claim on the land. Whites moved west onto Indian lands, and there was conflict when Indians refused to withdraw from the land.

"Whites try to convince Indian people that the old ways are gone, and they must change. Indian people must adopt the white man's lifestyle, growing crops and raising cattle. To begin the process, they tell Indian people they must move to reservations where whites will protect them and provide for them. This has never worked. Some Indians agreed to move to reservations, but food was always short, and the process of helping Indians to learn farming and ranching is never provided.

"Indians on reservations became hungry and frustrated, so they left the reservations to follow the buffalo. Some angry Indians, mostly young men, raided white farms and ranches and wagon trains. The army was called in, and fighting began. Many whites believe that if Indians will not accept that the old ways are gone and refuse to live on reservations, the problem will not be solved until Indians are finally defeated in battle and forced to change. If they still resist, they will be killed."

He held both her hands. "Winnie, not all whites believe this. There are many good white people. But these whites live mostly in the East where they have no contact with Indian people. It's mostly the white people in the West who want Indian lands who cause the problems." She pulled her hands from his.

"Do you understand?" he said.

"I hear what you say, but I not understand why white people think Indian people must give up places we have lived since the beginning."

He looked up into the black sky. He pulled her to him and held her, his face pressed into her hair. *How*

*can I explain more clearly that the problem here is not
primarily race, but greed? How to explain greed to her
when Indian people have no concept of greed?*

––––––

Bret and Winona sat their horses staring across the
grassy prairie at a large, high-walled stone structure that
sat on a low hill overlooking the river. Cannons sat at
corners of the roof and on parapets. Cacti grew on the
roofs of covered areas. Smoke from fires inside and
outside the walls rose in spirals in the still air.

"Bent's Fort," said Brett. He turned to her. "You say
you've never been here?"

"Never."

They rode at a walk toward the fort. Brett was
quiet. Twice he did not respond when Winona spoke
to him.

"Is something wrong?" she said.

Still he did not answer. He frowned. *Something is
not right. What is it?*

Brett pulled up abruptly when they were less than a
hundred yards from the fort. He leaned forward in his
saddle, staring. *My god! That's it!* He saw soldiers
walking about near the fort. A few tents were erected a
short distance from the walls.

"How could I forget! During the war between the
United States and Mexico in the 1840s, the old fort was
filled with soldiers, and the trade with Indians declined.
Then the fort burned in 1849, and Bent built this new
fort made of stone rather than sod like the old fort.
Trade with the Indians never did recover, and Bent
leased the new fort to the army in 1860.

"It's all coming back now. Chivington was at the fort last autumn and marched the hundred-day volunteers from the fort to Sand Creek. It's only a few miles from here." He slumped in the saddle. *I must have seen them on the trail that first day just after they left the fort.*

"My god. How could I have forgotten? There will be people here at the fort who know about the massacre at Sand Creek. Some of them might have been there. They could have seen us at the village."

Winona waited, staring at the fort. "Well, the soldiers see us now. Look."

Several soldiers at the tents and under the walls stood rigid, looking toward the two strangers.

He nodded. "Right. Let's go in. They'll be suspicious of people who look at the fort and turn away." They walked their horses toward the fort. Soldiers watched them come.

At the entrance to the fort, they saw three wagons outside the entrance. Oxen and horses grazed on a patch of dry grass nearby. Eight men huddled around a cooking fire watched Brett and Winona. One bewhiskered old man in buckskins stood and waved.

Brett hesitated, frowning, studying the wagons. He motioned to Winona with a nod, and they rode to the wagons. The men eyed Winona as they approached.

"Git down, pilgrim, we got coffee," said the old man. Brett and Winona dismounted, and Brett accepted the proffered mug. "We was just talking, me and th' boys, now what are these two about? A well-dressed young man and a Indian woman. You see, we like to guess and bet. As we watched you comin', I bet uh dollar you was a gov'mint man and she was your interpreter. Bobby here," nodding toward a middle-aged man who acknowledged the remark with a grin, "Bobby bet uh dollar you bein' a gov'mint man goin' to Santa Fé on gov'mint business, and she is your, uh, friend," followed by a broad grin and a glance aside at his smiling amigos, "and your interpreter."

Brett sipped his coffee. "Well, you aren't too far from the truth, though both of you lose your dollar. I'm with the railroad survey team investigating the prospect of building a railroad through the Southwest to California."

"Uh, railroad?" said another man at the fire, frowning. "That would sure finish the wagon trade."

"It wouldn't happen for a very long time, if ever," said Brett. "I see your loaded wagons. Are your goods for Santa Fé?"

"Yep," said Whiskers, smiling broadly, his chest puffed out. "We expect to be th' first wagons since the end of th' war. At least, th' war's just about over. We got no idea what sort of welcome we'll get, but I'm countin' on th' good people of Santa Fé wanting to get on with business."

Brett frowned, pondered. "When do you leave?"

"First light tomorrow. I expect we'll be on th' road before sunrise." Grins all around, a few good-natured frowns followed by smiles.

"Well, good luck with it. Santa Fé is going to be happy to see you fellows." Bret offered Whiskers his empty cup.

"Hope you're right," said Whiskers. He took the cup, clapped Brett on the back.

"You can bet on it," said Brett. He and Winona mounted and rode toward the fort entrance. Inside the fort, soldiers watched them ride by, their faces betraying neither welcome nor hostility. Brett and Winona dismounted, looked around.

"Winona!" Brett and Winona started at the shout. The speaker, a man dressed in buckskins, walked to her.

Winona relaxed, smiled. "George, it is good to see you." She turned to Brett. "This is George Bent. He is old friend. We see him at Sand Creek, but had no chance to talk with him or introduce him to you."

Bent nodded. "I remember." He frowned at Brett.

"Brett my friend," said Winona, "a good man who is friend of Indian people."

Bent relaxed, nodded again. "We will need good white friends in troubled times ahead. There will be war and death on both sides. I will try to prevent this, but I am only one man." He looked at Winona. "I ride north today. Are you okay to be here? There could be problems. After Sand Creek, the army is going to be busy. Our people will not be safe anywhere."

"Will you be safe?" said Winona.

"The army knows me. I have worked with them. I don't think they will harm me. They know I am white, but they also know I am Cheyenne." He pointed at Winona. "And so are you. Be careful. As for me, I will do what I can. I will talk with my people and try to reason with them. I know what the future holds for us. The whites are like locusts invading our country. They will increase; they will not go away. I will try to convince my people that we must find a way, we must find a new way."

"Be safe, George," Winona said. "I hope we see you again."

Bent nodded to her, stepped back, nodded to Brett,

then turned and walked toward the rooms along the inner walls.

————

Before he left the fort, George Bent arranged for Brett to meet with the army commander who assigned him a room. At the major's question, Brett repeated his claim to be with a railroad survey team. He hoped the major and other army officials would be too consumed with Indian affairs to be concerned with anything of such mundane subjects as a railroad survey.

The major expressed interest in the prospect of a railroad survey, but admitted he knew nothing of it. He said he would like to know more. "Let's talk tomorrow," the officer said. "I'll find you." Brett nodded in agreement, fearful since the major seemed to be sincere in his interest.

Brett and Winona walked their horses to the corral, quickly fed and watered them, trying to ignore the curious looks of troopers. Brett exchanged pleasantries with soldiers, annoyed that though they spoke to him, they watched Winona's every move. Brett focused on the horses and gritted his teeth, determined that he would finish this day without a brawl. He knew something of the hunger of young men, and these men had been deprived of the company of women for months.

Leading their horses from the corral, they tied the reins to the rail just outside their door. They carried saddles and goods from the packhorse into the room, dropped everything in a corner. They looked around. The room was empty but for two beds of wooden frames and rush mattresses. Brett decided that it probably was a spare storeroom, now unused.

"I need to rub the horses down," he said. "I'll just be a few minutes." He kissed her and went outside. Slowly rubbing the horses with a rag, he looked around. The fort interior was quiet but for the low conversation and occasional laughter of a few scattered troopers and tradesmen.

He opened the door and found Winona waiting. She put her arms around his waist. "I afraid. What we do now?"

He pulled her to him, rested his chin on her head. "I don't know, sweetheart. I'm exhausted. Tomorrow we'll talk. I'm a bit uneasy about this place. You heard what Bent said. I think we'll be moving on pretty soon. The major is too interested in us. I'm afraid he may ask me questions about the railroad survey I can't answer."

She pulled back, frowning. "What is 'sweetheart'?"

He smiled, kissed her lips lightly. "It means I love you with all my heart. Do you understand?"

She ducked her head, leaned against his chest. "Yes, I think so."

He raised her chin and kissed her. "Now we must sleep. Tomorrow we'll talk."

Brett pulled their beds together while Winona spread saddle blankets on them. They lay on the beds and pulled up covers. She reached over and rested her hand on his chest. He took the hand and held it.

Brett stared at the dark ceiling for what seemed an eternity, but was actually only minutes until he heard her breathing evenly and deeply. *I simply do not understand. Why am I here? Is this real? Or am I in my bed at home, dreaming? It makes no sense. I am thrust together with a woman who I love dearly, but is she real? Or is she only a beautiful spirit in my imagination? If she is real, and I have really been transported back in time, can I take her with me when I return to my own time and place? Can I return? Can I will a return? Or am I trapped in my obsession with the past?*

This can't be real. Think, man! I was at Sand Creek. I talked with Black Kettle. And now I'm at Bent's Fort. I talked with George Bent. But there is no mention of Brett Davis in the published histories of Sand Creek or Bent's Fort! He rolled his head violently side to side. *Maybe I am mad.*

He rubbed his face roughly and turned on his side. He lay still, eyes open, his mind racing. After an hour, he closed his eyes, and he slept.

———

Brett awoke with a start by a whinnying outside the door. He sat up, pulled his six-shooter from the holster hanging on the bed frame. Standing, he went to the door and slowly opened it. Bright moonlight illuminated the fort's interior and outlined the three horses at the rail. There was no sign of any people about. He looked through the open gates eastward and saw the faintest glow at the horizon.

He backed into the room and closed the door gently. Going to Winona's bed, he stooped beside her. "Winnie," he whispered.

Her eyes opened wide, and she sat up abruptly. "Wha—"

He put a finger to her lips. He whispered, "It's okay. It's okay. We need to leave. Now, before others wake up. I don't feel good about this place. I'm afraid questions are going to be asked today that I can't answer. The railroad survey thing won't hold up if they ask for details. I'll saddle the horses while you load the packhorse."

She threw back the cover, stood and rolled up the blankets while he picked up the saddles and went to the door. He looked outside, squinted, saw no shadows in the gloom that might suggest a person. Through the open gate, he saw the clear sky above the eastern horizon just beginning to lighten. By the time he finished saddling the horses, Winona had loaded the packhorse with the little they owned, a few bits and pieces of her clothing and some cooking gear.

They mounted, wrapped blankets around their shoulders, and rode at a walk toward the fort gate. Brett looked back into the fort interior and saw a single soldier at the far end of the parade, hitching up his suspenders, watching them as they rode through the gate.

Just outside the gate, Brett pulled up, looked toward the Santa Fé teamsters' camp. The firepit still smoked, but the wagons were gone. Brett frowned, staring at the wagon tracks in the dry grass, sparkling with last night's dew.

Winona leaned toward him. "Honey?" she said.

"Winnie, we're going to Santa Fé."

———

Brett and Winona rode behind the last of the three Santa Fé wagons. The teamsters had hallooed and shouted when they saw the couple riding up behind them an hour ago. The only proviso Max, the whiskered leader, imposed on their joining the group was Brett's confirmation that he was armed and would use his guns to help protect the cargo if it came to that.

"I feel good about this, Winnie," said Brett. "Nobody's going to know us in Santa Fé, and the teamsters here don't care about our past, just who we are now. And I've always been interested in the Santa Fé trade."

He told her at some length about the trade on the storied Santa Fé Trail between Missouri and New Mexico, beginning in 1821. While trade grew each year thereafter, the volume of traffic on the trail increased dramatically after the United States acquired the territory that included Santa Fé at the end of the Mexican War. As forts were established in the West to protect traders and settlers, the increased military demand for goods further stimulated traffic.

The trade was two-way. Caravans that formed in Missouri carried clothing, cloth, household goods of all sorts. Eastward, wagons carried silver coins, furs, processed gold, wool, and herds of mules. Missouri became famous as a source of mules for American farms. Mexican silver coins for years circulated as legal tender in and around Missouri.

Following Brett's discourse, they rode for some time in silence, Winona staring at her horse's head. "Do you understand?" said Brett.

"Yes, I think so." She turned to him. "But something I don't understand. You say we got to be careful because somebody wonder who we are and ask questions. We don't do nothing wrong. Why we have to be careful?"

"That's a very good question, sweetheart, something I have struggled with and still can't answer. I guess I have been extra cautious since Sand Creek. I'm afraid somebody, somehow, is going to find out I claim to be from the future. Maybe that won't cause trouble, but I don't know. If they don't accept my explanation, they might think I am mad and should be put away somewhere. Does that make sense?"

"Hmm. I understand." She frowned, staring at her horse's head. She turned to him. "Honey Brett. If I hear you say something you not supposed to know, I gonna touch my nose, like this." She touched the tip of her nose with an index finger.

He smiled. "Okay. I'll remember that. But how will I know you're not saying, 'kiss me here'."

She shook her head. "You listen me."

———

The camp was on a narrow flat covered by dry grasses. Thin patches of snow lay under short juniper trees and acacia shrubs. Low mountain ranges ran along each side of the flat. Brett and Winona sat with the teamsters around a large campfire. They ate strips of roasted venison from the deer killed by Brett that afternoon.

"Mmm-umm! That's good," said a teamster. "We don't usually take th' time for huntin' meat. Glad to have you with us," he said, pointing the chunk of meat at Brett.

Max chewed the last bite of his venison, wiped hands on his trousers and looked up at Brett. "You say you never been to Santa Fé?"

"Nope. The railroad survey never took me that way. Going now more from curiosity than work. No railroad is likely to go that far south. You've been there many times, I suppose."

Max looked up at the dark sky filled with twinkling stars. "Oh, yeah. I been, let's see..." His head nodded as he counted the visits. "I been there fourteen times."

"You ever get bored with the trip and the town?"

"Bored?" He smiled, looked at Winnie. "Oh, no, and I'll keep coming back, as long as I can sell my goods and th' señoritas will dance with me." He turned to the grinning teamsters. "Eh, boys?" Murmurs of agreement.

He leaned toward Brett. "It's different there. Not uptight like in th' States. People there know how to relax, have a good time, not worry."

"Did you ever visit Tules's place?" Brett said.

Max's eye opened wide. "Tules? You know about Tules?"

Winnie cleared her throat and tapped the end of her nose.

Brett frowned, glanced aside, back to Max. "I, uh, heard about her in St. Louis. She has quite a reputation."

Max grinned broadly. "Yeah, all th' traders know about her. Yeah, I've been to her place. I only play a couple of hands and always lose everything. Word is that she's th' best card dealer in the country, and I believe it. Course, there's other things to do at her place." He looked aside at his grinning fellows, some nodding, almost drooling. "Word is that she's th' governor's mistress, so nobody messes with her."

Winona finished her venison, stood, and stepped toward the darkness.

"Watch out for the thorns on that acacia, missy, right there in front of yah," called Max. She waved over her shoulder, walked past the acacia, and disappeared behind a low juniper.

Max leaned toward Brett. He spoke softly, conspiratorially. "If you want to go to Tules's, I'll take yah. Just leave th' little woman someplace. She wouldn't be interested or welcome. You understand."

"I understand."

"Damn, I git excited just talking about it, Tules's. She's got some of th' prettiest women this side of the Mississippi working for her in th' back rooms. Damn!"

Brett and Max looked up to see Winona walking back to the fire circle. "Where we sleep?" she said.

They went to the back of a wagon where Max had told them to stow their saddlebags and pannier. Pulling out blankets and saddles they used for hard pillows, they walked to the edge of firelight and rolled out the blankets.

They took off coats they had bought from Max, laid them on the blankets for added warmth. Removing boots, they lay down and pulled up blankets. She moved close to him, spoke softly. "What is Tules?"

He spoke into her ear. "Tules's is a place where men go to gamble."

"He say there other things to do at her place."

"Yeah. It's also a brothel. Do you know 'brothel'?"

"Is it same as 'whorehouse'?"

He snorted. "Yeah, same thing. Where did you hear that?"

"From white man I live with. Anytime he mad at me, he say if I don't be good, he gonna send me to whorehouse. Sarah, his wife, tell me about whorehouse."

"Max said he would take me to Tule's if I wanted to go."

She frowned. "You want to go?"

He smiled.

She pushed on his chest. "You go if you want to. Maybe I have fun with men here."

"Then I'll have to shoot every one of 'em."

She put her hand to his cheek, a light slap. "Oh, you think you so bad."

"Oh, I think you so good." He squeezed a breast, ran his hand down her back, and pulled her to him.

"No," softly, "you make too much noise." She pushed him away, snuggled, and pulled up the blanket.

———

"There she is, amigo." Brett and Winona stood with Max beside the lead wagon. They had pulled up on the height at the first glimpse of Santa Fé below. Beyond the town, a broad plateau marked by a scattering of green evergreen bushes and shrubs and patches of dirty snow. On the right, craggy foothills of the mountain range that overlooked the town.

Even at this distance, Brett was impressed that the town was, as so often described in the literature, a collection of hovels. *Now I regret having read so much about Santa Fé. As much as I looked forward to coming here, I have a hard time grasping the romance of the town rather than the reality.*

He started at Max's voice. "Three years since I been here," said Max, staring below. "Glad to be here again, one of my favorite places anywhere." He turned to Brett. "Th' more I talk with you about Santa Fé, th' more I git the impression you been here before. You sure you ain't been here?"

Winona punched an elbow into Brett's ribs as she repeatedly tapped her nose.

Brett turned away from Max, unable to suppress a smile. Sobering, he turned back to him. "Never, just read a lot and talked with teamsters back in Missouri." Max stared at Brett, waiting for more, but Brett looked blankly at him.

"Okay! Let's move," Max shouted to the others who had pulled up behind the lead wagon and got down to look at the town. Now they hurried to their wagons, some climbing up to seats and others to the lead yoke, waiting for Max to pull out.

Max pulled up to his wagon seat, gave the okay to his pard who stood beside the lead yoke. "Come up!" called the teamster and lightly punched the ox beside him with a stick. The team leaned into the yokes, and they were off. Max sat with his foot on the brake, ready for the downhill.

Brett and Winona mounted and followed the third wagon.

———

Winona and Brett strolled on a dusty Santa Fé road at dusk. On both sides of the road, men were lighting lamps attached to store fronts. They passed shops and saloons where locals lounged on the walks, chatting, laughing, smoking. Women puffed on cigars as comfortably as their men. Winona frowned at Brett.

"Would you like one?" he said. She wrinkled her nose.

"Hey, Brett! Winona!" They turned to see Max and three others striding across the road. "Wait up!"

"You were interested in Tules's. We're goin' there tonight. I'm closing a deal with my buyer right now. Got a good price. After some supper, we're goin' over to celebrate. Come with us." He glanced aside at Winona. "Uh, I..."

"Yeah, I suspect they don't welcome Indians," Brett said.

"That's about it, yeah. Also, uh, women don't usually go there, unless they work there."

"I'm not leaving Winnie alone in this town."

"Ah, well. If you can think of something, we'll see you there." He waved, and the four strode away, chatting and gesturing, laughing.

Winona took Brett's arm. "You can go. I be okay."

"Nope. Out of the question." He paused, pondered, frowned, staring down the road. "C'mon." He took her arm, and they walked across the road toward a line of shops.

———

Brett and Winona stood on the walk at dusk before a brightly lit Tules's. Patrons walked in and out, most pausing to stare at Winona.

She wore a long red dress that almost covered her slippered feet. A long necklace of a half dozen strands hung to her waist, and she wore two pins attached to the dress just below the neckline. Her hair was coiled high on her head, held there by a large orange comb. A multi-colored feather protruded from the top of the coil.

Winona returned the stares of passersby, trying to

project a look described by Brett. He had called it "haughty".

Brett leaned over. "Ready?"

She lifted her chin, blinked, nodded ever so slightly. "Yes." She leaned over, whispered, "Am I haughty?"

"Indeed you are."

He took her hand, placed it under his elbow, and they walked in, passersby stepping aside. One dressed as a gentleman nodded, almost a bow.

Just inside the door, a portly man dressed in vest and bowler hat barred their way. "Sorry. We don't take no——"

Brett held up a hand. "Hold it right there. I don't want you to embarrass yourself. This is Princess Petrushka of Azerbaijan. She is visiting the United States, and I am detailed by the government to show her some of the leading sights of our great country. She read about Tules's in Washington and wished to visit. We have endured a long journey to come here."

Open-mouthed, the man looked down and stepped aside. Dozens of patrons who had witnessed the confrontation also moved back as Brett and Winnie stepped in. Winnie looked about, blinking, chin slightly raised, haughty.

They walked past the dance floor and gaming tables toward the bar. Patrons paused, holding drinks, leaning against tables, watching Brett and Winona. At the bar, Brett ordered aguardiente. He had always been curious about the local whiskey, also called Taos Lightning, and now was about to sample it at the source. The bartender poured it, pushed the glass to Brett, and went to another patron down the bar.

Winnie looked about nervously. "Winnie?" Brett said softly.

She wrinkled her nose. "I don't like haughty."

He smiled. "Just a few minutes more, and we'll leave. I'll finish my drink, or it will finish me. This stuff is about to take the top of my head off. It's well-named, fire water."

"Brett! Winnie!" They looked up to see Max and half a dozen others who had just come through the door. Brett held up a hand, looking around nervously as the teamsters strode to the bar.

They stopped, looked Winnie up and down. "My, my, my, you look like uh princess or somethin'. Hey, you don't need to dress up to come to Tules's. Anyway, I gotta tell yuh, I like th' skins better."

Bowler hat had watched this from his station near the door. He beckoned to three others, and they strode to the bar. "I knew she was uh Indian," Bowler said. "Now you bunch git outta here. All of yuh.!"

"Hey," said Max. "Hang on there. We just got here, and I been lookin' forward to Tules's the last three years. I ain't goin' nowhere!"

Bowler hat and another man grabbed Max's arms and began to move him away from the bar. Suddenly a teamster pulled his pistol and pointed it in Bowler's face. Bowler dropped his arms and backed off. Accomplices rushed to his aid, and the fight was joined.

Traders in the bar, most of whom had been drinking for hours, shouted and joined the fight on the side of their brethren. Employees rushed from behind bars and came from other rooms and were quickly caught up in the melee. A shot was heard, then another.

Brett took Winnie's arm firmly, moving her to the

door, pushing through wrestling and shoving bodies, most blows by the mostly drunk patrons punching air. Once outside, Winnie and Brett ran in the middle of the road, stumbling and laughing. They stopped, looked around, and went to a dark space between two shops where they tore off the princess clothing and dropped it.

"Yeah, I like the skins better," he said. Luckily, she had worn the buckskin dress under the princess clothing.

CHAPTER 4

The days following were lazy days as Brett and Winona strolled the streets of Santa Fé, coats buttoned and collars up against the cold, enjoying the occasional sunshine. They often sat in the plaza, watching passersby who ambled, paused, passing the time, or walked briskly, eager to be someplace else.

They sat one day at an outdoor cafe, the weak sun almost warm in the still air. He looked up into the bare branches of the tall cottonwoods, sighed heavily.

She reached over to take his hand. "Time to go?" she said.

"You read my mind. It's safe enough here, but there's nothing for us here. I've got to be doing something."

He sipped his coffee, looked blankly across the plaza to the shops opposite. *Where to go? Texas? Do I have enough cash to finance a cattle ranch? A cattle drive to a Kansas railhead town? Doesn't sound promising at the moment. Later perhaps, but not now. California?* He racked his brain but could not come up with any useful information on what was going on in California in 1865, except it was in the waning years of the gold rush. And he knew nothing of how they would travel to California. *Should we find a town where I could apply for a teaching job? But how would I explain my credentials?*

"We'll go east. The army will be aggressive for some time against the plains tribes. There's nothing we can do there, so we'll stay out of trouble by leaving the region."

———

Max invited them to travel with the wagons on the trip eastward. They would leave as soon as he had accumulated a load of silver and furs. And mules. The teamsters were still bickering with local ranchers for a herd. It seems the army's demand for mules had raised the price and reduced the supply. Brett pondered, but decided they would be safe enough on their own, and he was finished with Santa Fé. He and Winnie said goodbye to Max and the others.

They left at first light on a cold January morning. They had loaded two packhorses with foods and some little trade goods or gifts if opportunity or necessity should arise. Reaching the pass at the top, they paused to look back on the town below. Somehow the town was more picturesque, even romantic, at a distance than up close.

He stared below, grim. "I hope we're not making a mistake."

She reached over and touched his hand. "We be okay. We together."

———

They rode in a rolling prairie covered with dry grasses and scattered sagebrush. In the distance, a faint brown image was etched on the skyline. If they didn't know they were passing Bent's Fort, it would seem a rocky outcropping.

"I hope George is okay," Winona said. "He is white and Indian, so people might think him friend or enemy."

"He'll be okay. He's a smart man, seems to calm people, not get them angry." *Well, usually.* He did not tell her that after their conversation with him at the fort, Bent was a member of bands that fought troops in a series of battles. Nor did he tell her that Bent eventually became an interpreter for the government and was seen as an enemy by his Cheyenne people. Nor did he tell her about Bent's writings in the twentieth century when he stated eloquently that the real savages in the Indian-army troubles were the soldiers.

George Bent was a complex figure, perhaps the best example of the conflict between the old way of life and the new way described by the agents and army officers, a new way which never materialized. *Maybe someday I'll tell her more about George Bent. His life symbolizes the agonizing hope of the Indian people and the loss of that hope. I'll tell her someday, not now.*

———

Brett and Winona huddled under a rocky overhang at the mouth of a dark cave. The rain that had driven them to the overhang fell in torrents, blowing sheets into the mouth of the cave, wetting their coats and blanket coverings and driving them deeper into the cave.

The storm slackened, and visibility improved. "Look." Winona pointed down the slope below the cave to a copse of spruce trees. There in the dark shade of the trees stood three antelope, heads hanging, not moving, waiting out the storm.

"Oh, my," Brett said softly. Staring at the antelope, he reached for the rifle he had leaned against the wall when they first found refuge in the cave. He leveled on an antelope and fired. The animal lurched and dropped as the others bolted, ran from the shelter of the trees to the open prairie.

Brett lowered the rifle and leaned it against the wall. "Here's a break from the rabbit meals that you like so much," he said, smiling.

"You know I don't—"

She stopped, looked wide-eyed at Brett. A snuffling, a low, rumbling growl, issued from the dark tunnel behind them.

"Bear," said Winona softly. She took his arm, pushing him toward the cave entrance. He pulled away, stepped back into the cave.

"Brett! Wha—"

He held up the rifle he had retrieved, then hurried to catch up. They scrambled and slid from the cave entrance down the hill. At the bottom, they stopped and looked back toward the cave. Nothing. The bear had returned to its hibernation.

"Whew," said Brett, wide-eyed.

She smiled. "You never hear bear this close?"

"No, I never hear or see bear this close, and I don't want to see or hear bear any closer."

The heavy rain lessened to a drizzle, and they shook the drops from their coats and blankets. Brett confirmed that the horses were still tied, luckily a distance from the antelope, where they had left them when they fled to the cave at the first burst of thunder. They walked to the downed antelope.

She went to the packhorse, opened a sack and pulled out a knife. She came back and offered the knife to Brett.

He recoiled. "Uh, well..."

"You never do this before?"

"No."

She laughed, dropped to her knees beside the carcass, and proceeded to dress the antelope expertly, slicing and carving. Brett watched, relieved and impressed.

While Winona was busy with the antelope, Brett dug in the debris at the foot of the trees to collect enough dry tinder to start a fire. He scooped out a fire pit, pressed the tinder tightly together, and placed it in the center of the pit. On his knees beside the fire pit, he reached into a pants pocket and pulled out three matchbooks. Replacing two of the books, he opened the third. It contained but two matches. He tore off one, struck it against the abrasive strip, and the match head burst into flame. He applied it to the tinder, igniting the dry needles. Picking up sticks from a stack beside the fire circle, he carefully placed them over the burning tinder.

"Brett." He looked up to see her staring at him. She lay the knife down and walked to him. "I see you do this before, but never ask you about it." She stared at the matchbook.

"These are called matchbooks." He showed her the

matchbook, with the picture of the Tea With Me shop where he had picked up the matchbooks. "They were in my pocket when I was transported from my time to your time. I always carried these when I went camping. I used them to start fires. Matches were invented before my time and improved over the years." He opened the matchbook and showed her the two matches. "This stuff on the head will burst into flame when the match is rubbed against stone or some other hard material. I won't show you now. I have only these few left. Be sure to watch me when I make another fire. When these are gone, you'll have to teach me how you make fire your way."

She smiled, leaned into his face. "I can do that."

He took her face in his hands and kissed her, looked into her eyes. *Winnie. Sweetheart. If I am to remain in your world, you will have to teach me many things. You will have to teach me to become a Cheyenne. If we are ever to go to my world, oh, what things I will show you!* He sobered, bent to work on making a fire.

When she was finished gutting the antelope, she sliced off two sizable chunks from the hindquarters, lay them on the carcass. She stood, motioned Brett to come with her. Rummaging in debris under the trees, they found forked sticks and a sturdy bough from which she fashioned a spit. Spearing the chunks of meat on the sharpened bough, she placed it carefully on the forked sticks they had pushed into the wet ground on each side of the fire pit. She added short sticks to the fire, and they caught immediately, steam rising from the wet wood.

She straightened, flexed her back. "Now we wait," she said. "Not long, I think. I very hungry."

They watched the sun ball dropping toward the horizon, coloring the fleecy cloud layers shades of pink, red and orange.

"Look!" she said. A perfect rainbow, pastel bands melting into each other, slowly materialized, each end of the arc touching the ground. "When I was little, my mother say the place at bottom of a rainbow is the happiest place. She always say she want to go there." She looked at him, sadly, it seemed. "Is there happy place we can go?"

"I hope so, sweetheart. We will look for it."

She sat beside him at the fire circle, warmed her hands over the flames. "Now tell me what you do in your time. You never tell me much."

He looked aside at her, looked into the flames. "I am a teacher. I teach history to young men and women. History is stories of what happened in the past. In particular, I teach about what happened in the American West, what happened before white people went into the country, how native people lived. People like you. And I talk about what happened after whites went into the West." As he talked, she leaned toward him, closer and closer, watching his face, until she pressed against his side.

He turned to her, and she kissed him. He put his arms around her and pulled her to him. He smiled thinly. "And then what happened?" he said.

"And then nice white man come into West and meet Cheyenne woman."

He kissed her cheek, and the tip of her nose. "And then what happened?"

She kissed his lips lightly. "Then she say, 'I very

hungry!'" She pulled away quickly, stood and went to the fire pit, laughing.

Impatiently, they feasted on the half-cooked antelope meat. Brett checked the hobbled horses, and they made their bed on a layer of dry leaves and soft detritus. Building up the fire and piling more dry sticks at the fire circle, they crawled into bed. She pulled up the blanket and snuggled against him.

She put a hand to his cheek. "And then what happened?" she said, softly.

———

Winona awoke at a low sound of muffled conversation. Pushing back the blanket, she sat up, looked around in the weak light of dawn. She was startled to see Brett standing beside the hobbled horses, facing six mounted Indians, two at the front holding loose bows with arrows pointed at him.

She threw the blanket back, jumped up and ran toward the Indians, shouting and waving her arms. A horseman at the back of the group slowly pulled a rifle from its scabbard and held it at his side, watching her come and moving his horse slightly apart from the others. The bowmen kept their arrows pointed at Brett.

Winona came up to the Indians. She shouted at them in Cheyenne, angrily, waving her arms, pointing at Brett. The horsemen frowned, looking at each other. They mumbled hesitantly, looking from her to Brett. One of the Indians smiled, said something to the others. Two laughed lightly.

A rider spoke to Winona. She answered, and the Indians spoke to each other. Others spoke to her. The conversation was light and cordial. The riders holding bows lowered them, dropped arrows into quivers. The warrior with the rifle, older than the others, slid it into the scabbard, said something sharply to the others. The young Indian who had spoken most with Winona said something to her, laughed, and all drummed their horses' bellies, laughing and yelping as they galloped away, sheets of spray erupting from the soaked grass.

Brett, wide-eyed, walked to Winona. "What in hell was that all about? I thought it was all up. I didn't know whether to pray or yell for you to come."

"I knew they were Cheyenne from their clothes. They boys, all except man with gun. Boys like to act like they are warriors, and they want to prove they brave. And they have seen some bad things from white men. They more scared than you."

"What did you say to them? Why did they laugh? Why did they leave?"

"I told them you were good man and friend of Indian people. I told them Indian people need to be friends with good white people. I told them to be men, and if they could not be men, they should go back to village for their mother's milk." She raised her chin.

"Whoa. A white man would have shot you if you had said that to him. I'm glad they thought you were funny and decided to be men."

He went to her and embraced her. "You saved my life. I wonder how many times you're going to have to do that. We're likely riding into trouble, no matter which direction we take."

———

After searching his memory of lectures and books, he decided that they should ride east and north, away from the turmoil in the western plains and away from the unrest in Texas. *Why not Kansas?* He was unsure of what they would find, but he figured it would be safer there than staying in the region where the army would clash for years with the plains tribes.

As they rode, Brett lamented not having paid more attention to Kansas in his reading and his lectures. He remembered that Kansas had been a battleground during the Civil War between factions supporting the Union and the Confederacy. He knew there were fierce differences, during and after the war, over the slavery question. The Civil War would not end for a few months, in April, but he reckoned that it was relatively quiet in the state now.

So what would they find here, in early 1865? He ticked off the western cattle towns in memory. Dodge City? Too early. The first Texas cattle wouldn't arrive in Dodge until the early 1870s. Ellsworth, east of Dodge, wasn't founded till the late 1860s. He couldn't remember the year.

That left Abilene, farther east. He recalled that the first Texas cattle arrived in Abilene in 1867, the same year the railroad reached the town. Surely the town was settled and established some years before that date.

They would ride to Abilene. He was immediately relieved with the choice. They would not have to search for a route to Abilene. Travel over the Santa Fé Trail, from Independence to Santa Fé, was disrupted little by the Civil War. Military use of the trail was heavy throughout the conflict, and traders' wagons continued to roll to Santa Fé. Indians, sensitive to the increasing presence of whites in their country, often attacked troops and traders on the trail.

After the Sand Creek massacre, conflict between Indians and military seemed to shift northward, giving some relief to Santa Fé traders who expected to benefit from relative peace in the region. The three wagons Bret and Winona saw at Bent's Fort would be among the earliest in an upsurge in Santa Fé commercial traffic.

As they rode on the flat prairie under a clear blue sky, Brett told Winona his decision. She listened, her face blank, staring at her horse's mane. She turned to him. "Ab-i-leen. I never heard it. What does it mean?"

Brett frowned. He recalled that most Indian place names have a meaning. He squinted, scouring his memory. "Ah, yes. It comes from the Bible. Do you know about the Bible?"

"I know Bible. Sarah, the white woman I lived with, read from Bible every day after supper, after the man went to bed. He didn't like Bible. He said it was a bunch of lies. She said she like New Testament better than Old Testament. She say Old Testament has very bad stories. She say New Testament tells good stories, about heaven where good people go when they die."

"Hmm. Well, if I remember correctly, Abilene in the New Testament means a grassy place. If what I have heard of the town of Abilene is right, it is on the prairie, a grassy place." *Interesting that the name Abilene is biblical since it becomes a devilish place as the first of the Kansas cattle towns.* He chuckled.

"What is funny?"

He explained.

"How do you know—" She frowned, pounded the

saddle horn with a fist. "Never mind; I know." He smiled.

They rode silently, each in their own world, sometimes nodding, eyes closed, then searching the prairie in all directions. A soft breeze blew, moving the knee-high grasses like ocean waves, bending, rising, laying out, flowing.

Winona reined up, spoke softly. "Brett." He pulled up, saw her staring northward off the trail. "Look," she said. He looked, squinted, saw nothing.

"What do you see?"

"Animals. Buffalo, I think."

They dismounted. Reaching behind his saddle, he pulled the binocular from the saddlebag. He scanned the prairie until he saw them. "Yes, small bunch, dozen or so, 'bout three hundred yards." He lowered the binocular, his hand shaking. It was the first buffalo he had seen in the wild.

"You shoot one. I no eat buffalo meat in long time."

He frowned. He had not even thought of shooting a buffalo. *But why not? Here I am on the prairie in 1865 where buffalo are still here in the millions. Why not? Not in my wildest dream did I ever think I would hunt buffalo.* "I'll try. But understand that this is all new to me. In my time, buffalo are not wild. Nobody hunts them. I hope you will not be disappointed."

"Our men always kill buffalo when they go after them. I *will* be disappointed if you don't kill one, but I will understand if you can't do with rifle what our men do with bow and arrow."

She jumped away when he tried to grab her, fending him off and laughing. When he stopped chasing her and simply stared at her, she came to him, took his face in her hands, and kissed him.

He sobered, put his arms around her and held her, staring over her shoulder at the prairie. *What am I going to do with this woman?* "What am I going to do with you?"

She leaned up, kissed his cheek, whispered in his ear: "You are going to shoot a buffalo for me."

"Hmm. Okay." He shut his eyes, trying to recall what he had read about buffalo hunting. "Okay. Here's what we'll do. I'll tie the packhorses to that bush there." He motioned to the bush with a nod, then pointed northward. "You ride slowly in that direction. That's upwind from the buffalo. I will ride in the opposite direction, downwind of the buffalo." He pointed. "I'll try to find a place to hide. The buffalo will get your scent and move in my direction."

"You not going to run buffalo?" she said, stifling a smile.

He frowned. "No, ma'am, I am not going to run the buffalo. I'll leave that to your men. Are we going to do this or not?"

"Yes, you do packhorses. I go." She mounted and set out at a slow lope. "I walk when I closer," she threw over her shoulder. "I do this before!" she shouted, laughing.

He shook his head, quickly tied the packhorses' reins to a bush, then checked his rifle, verifying that it was loaded. He pocketed another half dozen cartridges. He looked for Winona and finally saw her disappear down a shallow arroyo. Mounting, he kicked his horse into a slow lope in the other direction.

After a short ride, he dropped into a shallow depression, out of sight from the buffalo. Riding another five minutes, he slowed to a walk, then reined up when he judged he was roughly opposite where Winona would spook the herd. He looked around, spotted a low bush, and tied the reins. Pulling the rifle from its scabbard, he lay on the side of the depression, then inched his way up, pulling a blanket, the rifle, and binocular beside him.

He stopped at the top and searched the prairie with the binocular. He saw neither buffalo nor Winona, only the waving prairie grass.

He slumped and waited. He looked up at the squeaky, gurgling call of an unseen meadowlark, searched for the bird, but saw nothing. Then the meadowlark rose from the grass twenty feet away and flew across his view, the bright yellow breast brilliant in the sunlight.

He looked over the top for the buffalo and saw no animals. No buffalo and no Winona. A cool breeze chilled him, and he pulled the blanket tight around his shoulders. He closed his eyes, listened and heard nothing. *How seldom in my time do I hear silence.* His eyes closed, and he nodded.

His head came up abruptly, and his eyes opened. Raising the binocular, he scanned the meadow. *There!* The small herd walked slowly from behind a patch of boxwood shrubs, grazing as they moved ahead.

Suddenly all of the buffalo raised their heads and looked behind them. Brett moved the binocular and saw Winona riding slowly toward the bunch. The buffalo turned together and began walking away from Winnie and toward him. Then the animals in the lead walked faster, and some began to lurch forward.

He tensed, brought the rifle up on the top of the rise, pointing toward the approaching buffalo. He felt a throbbing, wondered whether it was his heart or his head. The buffalo broke into a lope, seemingly not overly alarmed by the slow-moving Winona.

Now the buffalo were a hundred yards away. *Should I fire now? Or wait to see if they will come closer? Or will they break away to the right and make the shot longer? Now?*

He sighted on a small buffalo on the near side of the bunch and fired. The animal stumbled and fell, tumbling and rolling while the other buffalo galloped ahead, disappearing into a shallow arroyo.

Brett stood, exhaled deeply. He waved to Winona who had galloped at his shot and now sat her horse beside the fallen buffalo. She did not respond to his wave. She was turned in the saddle, looking behind her.

Brett scooted down the slope, went to his horse, slid the rifle into the scabbard, and mounted. He had just cleared the top of the depression when he saw two riders, one leading another horse, approaching Winona. Brett kicked his horse to a gallop. He and the two horsemen came up to Winona at the same time. The men looked from Winona to the downed buffalo.

The two bewhiskered men, one middle-aged, the other older, wore rough, worn clothing and heavily sweat-stained broad-brimmed hats. Their burnt, creased faces suggested a rough life out of doors.

"I see you got one," said one of the riders.

"We did," said Brett. "You fellows buffalo hunters?"

"Not buffalo hunters, but huntin' buffalo," said the second rider. "Didn't know what to think when we saw her movin' up on the bunch we was watchin'." Both men stared at Winona, then at the carcass, back to Winona and then Brett. They were not smiling. Winona looked anxiously at Brett.

"There's plenty for all," Brett said. "We'll just cut off a chunk for supper and another for breakfast. Take the rest of it."

The men relaxed. "That's mighty neighborly of you," said the older of the two. "Just might give our whole bunch buffalo steaks for supper. On that point, unless you got other plans, why don't you two come and have supper with our outfit?"

"What outfit's that?"

"We got four wagons, headin' for Santa Fé. How about it?"

Brett looked at Winona. She looked blankly at him. "Santa Fé?" he said. "You're going to Santa Fé?"

"Yeah. We'll talk later, after we've fed ourselves. Gonna be gettin' dark before long, and we need to get this meat back to camp. You comin'?" He focused on Winona while talking to Brett.

Brett noticed the attention to Winona. He pondered, looked at Winona, back to the men. "Sounds good. We'll get our packhorses and catch up." He kicked his horse to a gallop, and Winona followed. The two men watched them a moment, then dismounted, pulled knives from belt sheaths and bent over the buffalo carcass.

Brett and Winona pulled up at the packhorses which shied at their approach. He dismounted and untied the reins from the bush.

"I don't understand about these men," said Winona. "Why we going their camp?"

Brett checked the packs on the packhorses, tightened the cinches. "I'm not too anxious to spend time with them, but it might be worthwhile to talk with them. If they are heading for Santa Fé, they might know something of Abilene. If so, they can tell us about the town, if there is a town. If there's no town, we'll have to change plans. Remember I asked Max about Abilene, and they bypassed it."

He mounted, and they set out at a lope.

Four wagons were arranged in a rough circle around two campfires. A sizable herd of oxen and some mules grazed near the wagons. Brett and Winona sat at a fire with the two men they had met on the prairie. Three men sat nearby, gnawing on chunks of buffalo steak; five more leaned against wagons, chatting and smoking. Pieces of buffalo meat skewered on a rod dripped juices into the low flames in the firepit.

One of the hunters, Ned, he called himself, wiped his hands on his trousers, smiling contentedly. "That was most welcome. First buffalo this season. In fact, first buffalo for me in years. Now." He pointed at Brett. "You asked if we were going to Santa Fé. I would like to think we are the first wagons on the trail this year. Wanted to get on the trail earlier, but somehow we got right in the middle of a ruckus between pro-slavery and anti-slavery people. We had to wait it out."

"That delay might be the reason you're not first on the trail. There's a party ahead of you, three wagons under a boss named Max."

The man slapped his leg. "Damn, thought we was first. I know Max. Good man. He must've left from some other town. We left from Independence. Oh, well, no problem. There'll be plenty of buyers."

"You have more men than Max," said Brett.

"We don't really need this many men, but a few of the boys here are also Santa Fé traders who are going along with us to see what sort of reception we get. If it's good, they will take their own wagons on the trail next season. The trade was pretty good during the war, but I expect it is really gonna take off, now that the war is dwindling down."

Ned addressed his conversation at Brett, but he mostly looked at Winona, as did his companion. She ignored the stares as she ate. When she finished eating, she wiped her hands on the grass at her side, leaned over and whispered in Brett's ear. He nodded, she stood and walked between two wagons into the darkness. The men lounging against wagons watched her, grinning and talking softly.

"What are you carrying?" said Brett.

"We're carrying pretty much what we've always carried, before and during the war," Ned said. "Cotton goods, blankets, linens, hardware, tableware, cutlery, some jewelry, gunpowder, clothing like trousers and shirts, coats. Hell, we even got some whiskey and champagne!"

"Quite a load. I suppose that's why you have that big bunch of oxen out there."

"Six yoke to the wagon," Ned said. "If all goes well this year, we'll use bigger wagons next year with more yokes in the team."

"You said you're carrying clothes. Would you have some men's clothes for my woman? She needs to get out of the buckskins."

Ned smiled. "Don't know 'bout that, friend. I thank she looks pretty good in skins."

Brett looked down, pondered. He looked up. "Do you have something? We bought a few things from Max, but they turned out to be too big, and she went back to the buckskins. She needs a couple pairs of pants and a couple of shirts. A hat, too, if you have hats. And she could use some new boots. Coats for both of us. We bought coats in Santa Fé, but they just about fell apart."

"Got it all except boots." Ned stood, walked to the nearest wagon. He reached into the wagon, pushed some bundles aside, pulled out four bundles and dropped them on the ground. Ned opened the bundles, and Brett sorted through the contents of each until he found what he needed.

"Looks good." Brett wrapped everything in one of the coats. "I'll get my money." He walked to the wagon where his four horses were tied to wheels. Dropping the clothes on the ground, he moved around his mount, away from the campfires, and pulled his wallet from the saddlebag. He had not touched the wallet since discovering the bills in it at the 2022 camping place.

Opening the wallet, he confirmed that the bills were still there. He pulled out the price of the clothes and replaced the wallet. He looked over the horse's back to see half a dozen men staring at him. He walked to Ned, handed him the bills.

Ned's eyes opened wide. "Whoa, you got the new bills. I saw some in Independence, but never had any myself. I'll have to show these to the boys." He walked to the campfire, studying the bills. The other men came over to him, and he showed them the bills. Some of the men glanced aside at Brett. The bunch broke up, some to lean on wagons, a couple who walked past wagons into the darkness in different directions. Ned and some others sat at the campfire, rolled cigarettes and smoked.

Brett walked to the campfire and sat on the ground beside Ned, warmed his hands. "Have all your boys been on the Santa Fé Trail before?"

"Yep. We all know the country ahead pretty good."

"Then you've probably come into contact with the Indians who live thereabouts."

"Yep. Never had any trouble with 'em. We've even traded with 'em."

"Have you heard about Sand Creek?"

"North of Bent's, ain't it? What about it?"

Brett pondered. He told them about the massacre. The men standing beside wagons straightened, listening. They walked over and sat or stood near Brett and Ned. Soon every trader, except the two who had walked into the darkness to do their business, was gathered around, listening silently.

"You were there?" said Ned. "How's that?"

"I was there. I'm with a railroad survey team and just happened to be there when it happened."

"Me gawd," said one of the traders. "Does that mean trouble for us?"

"You know the country better'n I do," said Brett. "You're going to be traveling in Indian country, and the tribes are not happy. Just thought you should know."

The group was silent, digesting Brett's revelation. "Hey, boss," said a trader, addressing Ned, "why don't we take the Indian woman with us?" He turned to Brett. "You said she's Cheyenne, didn't you? Speaks English, don't she? She could be useful."

Brett, grim, looked up at the speaker. "She speaks

English. That's why she's with me. She's my inter-preter. She stays with me." He glared at the man until he turned aside.

The traders fell silent. They wandered away, mumbling, cursing, walking to their own wagons.

Only Brett and Ned remained at the fire circle. After a long moment, Brett turned to Ned. "Did you happen to pass through Abilene?"

Ned frowned. "Abilene? Came close. A few of us rode in. What do you know about Abilene?"

"Not much," Brett said. "Is there a town there?"

"Well, the people livin' there call it a town, but there's little to show for it. Some of the boosters say they expect the railroad to reach them in a year or two, also cattle from Texas to ship east. I wouldn't take bets on any of it.

"There's already trouble brewing between the people who expect to get rich from shipping Texas cattle east and farmers who don't look forward to herds of cattle tromping on their crops. Yeah, and most of the people don't look forward to a bunch of loud-talking, whiskey-guzzling, trouble-making Texans showing up in their town. But that's all guessing and all in the future. Right now, I'd say Abilene is quiet as a tomb."

Brett nodded. He looked past the wagons where Winona had disappeared into the darkness. *Where is she? Doesn't usually take this long to do her business.*

He looked into the flames as Ned pulled out a tobacco sack and offered it to him. Brett shook his head, watched Ned roll a cigarette, poke a stick in the fire, and light the cigarette.

Brett looked again into the darkness. He stood and walked past the wagons, stopped, listening as his eyes adjusted to the dark. He walked a bit farther, then stopped when he heard a muffled, groaning sound.

He walked slowly, quietly, toward the sound. He stopped when he saw in the moonlight a trader sitting astride a prostrate Winona, a hand over her mouth, the other hand under her dress. She struggled, her head jerking side to side.

The man's head came up sharply when he heard the cocking click of Brett's pistol as he pushed it gently against the man's temple.

"Easy, now, or I'll blow a hole in your head," Brett said softly. "Get up real slow, and put your hands up high where I can see 'em. Any funny business, and you're a dead man."

The trader stood slowly and stepped away from Winona, his hands held high. In the soft moonlight, Brett saw a terrified face.

"Are you okay," Brett said to Winona, without taking his eyes from the man.

"I'm okay." She raised up on an elbow. "Can I kill him?"

Brett had to resist smiling, his eyes fixed on the trader's face. "No, but I might if he gets out of line."

"Hey, man, it was just a little fun. I wasn't gonna hurt her. She's just uh Indian, fer god's sake!"

Brett brought the pistol handle down hard on the man's head, then landed a crunching blow to the jaw when he bent forward. The man crumpled and landed heavily on his back. "Son of a bitch," Brett mumbled.

Brett helped Winona stand, and they started to walk toward the wagons. Brett stopped, went back, bent down and tugged the teamster's boots off. He took

Winona's arm, and they walked between the wagons to the fire circle. Ned looked up.

"One of your men is out there," said Brett, motioning with a nod toward the darkness. "I think he's alive. He tried some funny business with Winona. If I see him around camp, I may kill him yet."

All the traders in hearing stared at Brett, frowning. Ned stood up, grim-faced. "Okay, okay. I'll have a look." He looked at Winona, back to Brett. He saw the boots. "What you doin' with them boots?"

"Instead of shooting your man, I took his boots. Does that make sense?"

Ned looked blankly at Brett, then at Winona's moccasin-clad feet. He motioned to two men nearby who had listened to the conversation. "You two come with me." They disappeared into the darkness.

CHAPTER 5

A weak moon, partially obscured by a thin filmy cloud layer, cast shadows of wagons and animals. The camp was quiet but for loud snoring from underneath one of the wagons. A horse hobbled near a wagon snorted, shook its head.

At their camp outside the wagon circle, Winona and Brett quietly rolled their beds and tied them behind the saddles of their hobbled horses. He pushed Winona's new clothes into the packhorse panniers. They wore their new coats, buttoned with collars turned up in the chill air. While Winona held the reins of the four horses, Brett removed the hobbles and pushed them into a pannier. He took the reins of his mount and the packhorses from Winona, and they walked their horses northward silently away from the wagon circle.

Passing behind a low rising and out of sight from the wagons, they mounted and walked their horses. After a couple of miles, they kicked the horses into a lope. They rode alternately at a walk and a lope until midday when Brett decided they were well away from the wagons.

"Nobody's likely to come looking for us," he said, "so we'll get back on the trail. Let's stop for some lunch first. Glad you saved that last piece of buffalo."

They dismounted, tied reins to a low sage. He sat beside the horses while she fetched a bag from the pannier and took out a large, cooked chunk of buffalo. She had pulled it off the roasting stick last evening after everyone had their fill of the meat. She dusted off a flat rock beside Brett and placed the chunk on it. Going back into the pannier, she took a knife and used it to cut slices from the chunk. She passed a handful of slices to him and took some for herself.

She sat on the ground beside him. They ate silently, only looking up to scan the prairie for movement.

"How are the boots?" he said.

"Okay. Too big."

She turned to him. "What is 'lunch'?"

He frowned. "Hmm. Lunch. Well, it's... uh, in my time, the meal at noontime is called 'lunch'. The meal in the evening is called 'dinner'. Some people call it 'supper'." He took a bite of the meat. "We eat three meals a day at pretty much the same time, when we get up, noon, and about six or seven o'clock. When do the Cheyenne eat meals?"

She thought a moment. "We eat when we hungry."

He smiled. "Makes more sense than our plan."

She finished a slice of meat, picked up another. She paused, the slice halfway to her mouth, looking at him. "We always leave places at night. I think you like ride at night."

He held up a hand, finished chewing. "We leave at

night because we could be in trouble the next day if we stay. And because horny men like what they see when they look at you."

She frowned, wiped her hands on the grass, pursed her lips and looked at him. "What's 'horny'?"

He laughed. "It means that bad men want to do bad things with you."

"You do those things with me."

He smiled. "When I do those things with you, honey, they aren't bad. They're good." He put a hand on her cheek and kissed her.

She leaned over and kissed him, and again. "Cheyenne people did not kiss until we meet white people and learn from them."

"Cheyenne people learned too many bad things from whites, like drinking alcohol, but when they learned to kiss, that was a good thing."

She rubbed the knife on grass at her side, cleaning it. "What is 'honey'? I thought it a sweet thing bees make."

"Well, it is that, but it's also a pretty woman who is so sweet I want to eat her all up." He lunged at her, pushing her over and landing on top of her. He kissed her, looking into her eyes.

She smiled, kissed him. "Watch out for knife. Honey." She still held the knife at her side.

He took the knife and tossed it aside. "Get the blankets," he said, "while I tend to the horses. Sweetheart honey."

———

Day after monotonous day, they rode on the Santa Fé Trail, clearly visible after use for many years. Brett recalled from the books that game along the trail almost disappeared during the early years of heavy use, but that was no longer true. For some reason he could not explain, game was plentiful now, and he admitted that his male ego was stoked with the knowledge that he was able to keep the camp in wild meat with no difficulty, mostly pronghorn antelope which were more plentiful than buffalo. The pronghorn also was more curious than buffalo, sometimes standing like statues, watching them. The meat supply was augmented by another buffalo he bagged with Winona's help.

And there was the occasional rabbit when larger game was absent. Winona screwed up her face when she had to roast a cottontail, but she ate her share. "I don't like rabbit," she said, glancing aside at him and smiling.

———

On a balmy morning, almost warm, they rode in the middle of the well-marked trail. The prairie was covered with a light snow that was fast evaporating as a vapor that rose, glistening, from the flat land.

Winona reached over and touched his arm. "Why you smile?"

He looked at her. "Hmm. I suppose because we're safe, we're not hungry, and we're alone."

They rode silently. "Well, not alone for long." They saw wagons ahead coming their way. Moving off the trail, they waited.

The teamster in the lead wagon pulled up and waved. "Mornin', folks."

"Morning," said Brett. "S'pose you're heading for Santa Fé?"

"Yes, indeed. First time since the war started. We got six loaded wagons. You see any wagons ahead of us?"

"We saw two parties, three wagons under Max, and four wagons under Ned. Didn't catch last names."

"That's a surprise. Two parties ahead of us. Thought we was first on the trail this season. Don't know Max. The second party would be under Ned Bromfield. Good man. I heard he was headin' out, but I hoped to be ahead of him. No problem. Oughta be plenty of buyers in Santa Fé hungry for our goods."

The teamster looked back and forth from Brett to Winona during the conversation. She still wore the buckskins. She had told Brett that she would change to the western clothes before they reached a town.

"I see you picked up some goods of yer own," the teamster said. "Purty little thang. Would you be willin' to do a little tradin'? You can have your pick from my goods in the wagon."

Brett lowered his head. *Not again. Why do I have to deal continually with morons whose small brains are between their legs?*

"Did you pass through Abilene?" Brett said.

The teamster looked from Winona to Brett. "Yep. Six days ago. Well, the trail don't rightly go through Abilene, but some of us rode over to have a look. You goin' there?"

"Yeah. Six days. Didn't realize we were that close."

"Not much there. A few stores, enough for the local

population of farmers and ranchers. Some people think the place has a future. Newest buildings is a saloon and a little hotel. Owner of the saloon said he's expecting the railroad and Texas cowboys to show up before long. Don't know about that. Pretty quiet little town right now."

Brett nodded, waved a goodbye, reined his horse around, and Winona followed.

"How 'bout that exchange I mentioned?" the teamster called.

Brett waved over his shoulder without looking back. He thought about flipping the bird but decided that the teamster might know what it meant. *I don't need more trouble. But if he says anything more, so help me, I'll shoot him.*

They had not ridden a hundred yards when suddenly shots rang out behind. Brett and Winona pulled up hard. They looked back and saw a large party of about two dozen Indians riding toward the wagons, firing as they came. Teamsters quickly wrapped lines on brakes, jumped down and hustled behind wagons, and returned fire.

Winona kicked her horse into a gallop toward the fight. Brett, wide-eyed, galloped after her, shouting, "Winnie! Winnie! What are you doing?"

She raced toward the Indians, shouting and waving an arm. Surprised, most of the Indians reined up and watched this mad woman riding hard toward them. One leveled his rifle on her and fired. A warrior shouted at the rifleman. Indians and teamsters alike, surprised at the spectacle of this strange woman galloping between the raiders and wagons, held their fire.

Winona reined up before the Indian party and

spoke loudly to them, waving an arm at the Indians, pointing at the wagons. Brett could only rein up short of the gathering and watch. The warrior who appeared to be the leader spoke to her.

Winona continued talking, pointing at the wagons. The leader responded, and they talked. She pulled back and walked her horse toward the wagons.

"Winnie!" called Brett.

She waved without looking at him. Pulling up at the wagons, she spoke to a teamster. Other teamsters walked to her, guns at the ready. After an exchange, the teamster nodded, and she rode to the Indians. She spoke to the leader as others nearby leaned in to listen. The leader nodded.

As Brett watched, Winona, followed by the Indians, rode to the wagons. She and a half dozen warriors dismounted, handed reins to others and went to the backs of wagons where teamsters waited. With Winnie acting as interpreter, teamsters pulled goods from wagons and passed them to the Indians. Warriors chatted with each other, smiling, admiring the blankets and clothes they held. They raised arms in thanks or goodbyes to traders who responded in like manner.

The Indians mounted, holding their plunder tightly. A warrior looked back, spoke loudly, and all the warriors laughed. They kicked their horses to a gallop, shouting and yelping. Teamsters looked at each other, breathing sighs of relief, some smiling and patting each other on backs, speaking to Winona.

Brett rode up, dismounted. He frowned at Winona.

"What?" she said.

"You're trying hard to get yourself killed, aren't you?" Brett said.

"Hey, man, she saved our lives," said a young teamster. Other teamsters added their approval, smiling at Winona.

She spoke to Brett. "I know they Cheyenne and Arapahoe. I just tell them it better to talk than fight. Nobody get killed, and everybody happy. They say okay. Brett, leader say he understand talking better than fighting. He say he think he gonna lose four five men in attack. But he lose nobody, and they have what they come for."

Brett turned to the teamster leader. "What about you?"

"We got one man shot in the shoulder, not bad. Another hand is tending to him back there." He motioned with a nod to a wagon. "I hate to lose any goods to thieves, but we got off good. Nobody killed, and it cost us a few pairs of pants and some coats and blankets. I'm satisfied, thanks to your woman there." He nodded toward Winona, then turned back to Brett. "Sure you won't let her come with us? I'll give you your choice of my goods." He smiled at Winona who could not stifle a smile.

"You don't own enough goods here or anywhere," Brett said.

"That's what I figured you'd say."

Brett and Winona mounted.

"Vaya con Dios," said the teamster, waving. Brett returned the wave as they rode away. He kicked his horse to a lope, and she followed.

They slowed and rode at a walk. "Winnie. Just before they rode off, one buck said something I couldn't understand, but he was looking right at me, and all the others laughed. What did he say?"

She ducked her head, smiling. "He say, 'that woman crazy, you better do something 'bout her.'"

————

Well, the teamster was right. Abilene is a pretty quiet little town. Brett and Winona sat their horses just outside Abilene, looking down the sole street. They saw the makings of the town described by the trader. A saloon, a small hotel, a few storefronts on each side of the road.

"This is a town?" Winona said.

"Doesn't look like much, does it? It's going to grow pretty fast in the next few years, filled with cows and cowboys and the railroad and cow pens. It's going to be fast, busy and dangerous. We'll be gone long before any of that happens."

She stared at him until he turned to her. "What?" he said.

"You still scare me when you talk like this. I know how you do it, and I believe what you say, but if anyone else hears you, they will call you a shaman or crazy."

He smiled. "I'll admit to crazy." He set out at a walk toward the town. "Let's see if we can find some lunch." They rode into the town on the single road, pulled up at The Prairie Flower Hotel, still reasonably new, judging from the condition of the woodwork and paint. Dismounting, they tied reins to the hitching rail. Brett unfastened the saddlebags and threw them over his shoulder. He went to the packhorses, removed panniers and lifted them.

Looking around, he saw three people total, a man on the boardwalk on each side of the road, and a third walking across the road. All three stared at him and Winona. The men's clothes she wore did not hide a fetching woman. Brett and Winona stepped up on the boardwalk and into the hotel front door.

The hotel lobby was deserted but for a middle-aged, well-shaven man sitting at a table behind the counter. He looked out of place, dressed in pressed trousers, crisp white shirt, and black string bowtie. He stood, stepped to the counter, looked the newcomers up and down, unsmiling, waiting.

Brett and Winona went to the counter. "I'd like a room," Brett said.

The man stared at Winona, then turned to Brett. "We don't take no Indians."

Brett looked at the ceiling, closed his eyes. He opened his eyes, fixed on the man. He spoke slowly, softly. "This is not 'no Indian'. This is my wife. She is with me. I am a cattle buyer. I have come to Abilene to see whether I want to buy Texas cattle here and ship them to market on the railroad, of which I am an investor, and which is coming to Abilene very soon. Do you want to be responsible for me telling my Texas friends that The Prairie Flower Hotel does not welcome cattle buyers and cowboys and perhaps we should ship from Ellsworth instead of Abilene? Is that what you want?"

The man listened to this, jaw hanging, rigid. Suddenly he awoke from his trance, opened the register, and offered a pen to Brett.

Brett stared at him a moment longer, then took the pen and signed the register. He looked up. "I believe there's a livery down the street behind that line of shops?" He pointed. "Near where they plan to build the train depot?"

The man recoiled, frowning. "Yeah. I thought you just rode into town. How'd you—"

Winona took Brett's arm, touched the tip of her nose with the other hand. "I'm hungry. Where we gonna eat?"

Brett looked aside at Winona, then at the clerk. "Do you serve food here?"

"We got a kitchen and dining room, but we're not servin' yet, maybe in a week or two. You'll have to go to the saloon, four storefronts that way." He pointed. "They have food there if you ain't particular, and not much to choose from. I eat there sometimes, and I ain't dead yet." He almost smiled.

Brett extracted his wallet from the saddlebag and handed the bag to the man. He pointed to the panniers at his feet. "Put these in the room for me and lock the door. We'll try the saloon." The man handed Brett a key, put the saddlebag on his shoulder, and hefted the panniers.

Brett and Winona walked through the front door. Outside, Winona stopped, waved a pointed finger in front of his face. "You say too much! You tell him what is going to happen, and he start to think you crazy or some kind of spirit. He may tell other people to watch out for you."

Brett smiled. "You're right. I need to be more careful."

He took her arm, and they walked on the boardwalk four storefronts to the saloon. He opened the door, and they stepped inside. They stood just inside the door while their eyes adjusted to the dark interior. Only one of the six tables was occupied, one man leaned against the bar, and the bartender stood behind the counter. All stared at the newcomers. It was deathly quiet.

The four men at the table held cards, forgotten for the moment while they focused on Brett and Winona. Brett returned the stares only a moment, then walked Winona to a table in the corner, pulled out a chair, and she sat down.

He went to the bar and spoke to the bartender. "Good day to you, sir," Brett said. "I was told at the hotel that you serve meals. I don't see a menu, so I'll just order two meals and a couple of beers."

"We don't serve—"

Brett raised a hand. "Hold it right there. If you're gonna say you don't serve no Indians, I'm gonna get a little impatient. I'm a cattle buyer and a railroad investor. Now, if that doesn't mean anything to you, I'll explain in some detail." He leaned forward, both hands on the bar.

The bartender looked at the four men at the table who had listened to the exchange. One nodded.

"Have a seat," the bartender said to Brett.

Brett turned, looked at the card table a moment, then walked slowly to his table and sat beside Winona. They leaned toward each other and talked softly. The four at the table nearby strained to hear their conversation, but failing that, they returned to their cards.

Winona tapped the tip of her nose. "You lie so good, honey," Winona whispered, "that I sometimes believe what you say. I think other people believe you, too. Be careful. You were a surveyor, now a cattle buyer. Somebody gonna catch you."

"You're right. I must be careful." He recalled that

he had said that a number of times lately. *I'm falling into this fantasy too easily. Fantasy? I don't know fantasy from reality. Am I going to have a chance someday to write about all this? Will I lose Winnie when the fantasy fades? Or will she be sitting beside me when I write about it?* He rubbed his face with both hands.

She touched his hand on the table. "You okay?" He nodded.

They looked up when the bartender set two beers on the table. He returned to the bar, picked up two plates of steak, potatoes, and beans which he brought and set before them without a word. He took knives and forks from a vest pocket and set them in the center of the table. He looked at Winona, frowned, walked back to the bar, glancing aside at the card table. All four card players had watched all this.

At that moment, the outside door opened, and three cowboys came in, laughing, talking loudly. One stopped and threw a cigarette back through the opening before closing the door. They went to the bar, talked with the bartender who poured drinks and set them on the bar. One of the cowboys raised his glass, emptied it and pushed it across the bar. The bartender refilled it. The three sipped the drinks.

They turned around, leaned against the bar, drinks in hand. Glancing around the room, they settled on Winona. They talked softly, smiling, staring at her, sipping their drinks.

Brett cut a slice from the steak, forked it into his mouth, and chewed. He added a fork of beans. He cocked his head. "Passable."

Winona leaned toward him, spoke softly. "I don't like the way those cowboys look at me."

Brett glanced at the group at the bar. They ignored him, still looking at Winona, grinning, talking softly. "You're going to have to get used to that, men staring at you. You're a pretty woman. There won't be many women around here of any sort, probably few, if any, young pretty women. I don't mind 'em looking, but if they try to touch, I'm gonna bang heads." He pointed a fork at her. "I gotta say this, too. Most of the men out here will think that because you're Indian, they can do whatever they want with you. Remember what happened at the wagons."

"Nothing happened."

"Okay. Almost happened."

Winona nodded. She ate silently, then stopped a fork of meat in midair and turned to him. "At hotel, you say 'wife.'"

"Hmm. Yeah. Listen. In this strange world, we don't know what's going to happen. I must do and say whatever seems necessary to get us through to the next place, and I don't know what the next place is going to be. Does that make sense?"

She looked down. "Yes, I think so."

He took her hand in her lap and held it. "Just bear with me. You know I love you with all my heart, and whatever I do includes you. I will never leave you."

She looked up, frowning. "But what if—"

"Mind if I sit down?"

They looked up to see a man standing behind a chair at their table. Brett glanced at the table in the corner, saw an empty chair and the three men there looking at them.

"Sure, have a seat," said Brett.

The man slid the chair out and sat. "Heard you say you're a cattle buyer."

Brett put his fork down and leaned back. "Yep."

"Where you from? Why're you in Abilene?"

Brett glanced at Winona. "North Texas generally, Fort Worth particularly. Half a dozen friends, ranchers, and I decided that we need to find a market for our cattle. Our cattle went wild during the war, multiplying like crazy. Heard about the railroad pushing west in Kansas and decided that by the time we're ready to drive our herds up, it should have reached Abilene. Sound about right?"

"It does. But if you're driving cattle to Abilene, why do you call yourself a buyer?"

Brett frowned, looked aside—*yeah, why?*—then looked back at the stranger. "I'll be staying in Abilene after my friends and I finish our drive. I'll buy out my friends and stay on to buy the herds that follow. You see, other ranchers in Texas will hear about what we're doing, and they'll follow our lead and drive north. By then, I'll know what's going on in Abilene, and the railroad should be in town. I'll buy their herds."

The man slumped in his chair, stared grim-faced at Brett. He straightened and leaned forward. "Sounds most interesting. You sound like a competent and nice fellow. And reasonable, I hope. So I should tell you what's comin' down in Abilene.

"I work for a man who is coming to Abilene to do exactly what you say you're plannin' to do: buy Texas cattle and ship back East on the railroad. He's a big man and has plenty of backing." He leaned forward. "And he don't like competition."

Brett stared at the man, searching his memory. *This*

sounds familiar. Who's he talking about? Joseph McCoy? The histories all give McCoy credit for establishing Abilene as the most important shipping point for Texas cattle. Maybe, but I don't recall that he was belligerent. Or that he had any serious competition. Or that the history of Abilene as a cattle town mentions Brett Davis.

"What's this man's name?" said Brett.

"You don't need to know his name. If you hang around, you'll find out soon enough. I wouldn't advise you to do that." He pushed his chair back, scraping noisily on the uneven wooden floor, stood and walked to the table in the corner. The three men there smiled, staring at Brett and Winona. The man sat, the four picked up their cards and returned to their game.

Brett and Winona finished their meal, and Brett finished both beers. He shook his head vigorously when he downed the last swallow, concluding that he was very thirsty since the beer tasted just slightly better than how he assumed horse urine must taste.

They stood and walked to the door. Brett waved to the bartender who replied with a curt wave, glancing at the table of card players who had paused their game to watch the pair leave.

The three cowboys at the bar stared at them until they reached the door. One of them emptied his glass, wavered, pointed at the door, and grinned.

Brett and Winona walked to the hotel. He counted four men walking on the boardwalks, two on each side of the road, heads down, seemingly in a hurry. Brett wondered where in Abilene was that important.

They stopped in front of the hotel. "Go up and

have a lie down," said Brett. "I'm taking the horses to
the livery. I won't be long."

She went inside while he untied the reins of the
four horses. He mounted and walked his horse, leading
the others. At the end of the storefronts, he rode around
to the back and saw the livery.

He pulled up at the corral beside the barn. The
structure was substantial, obviously built not so much
for the present, but in anticipation of a larger population and demand. The large corral was empty.

"Halloo, anybody there?" Brett called.

A boy walked from the barn. "Yessir. Got some
horses for me?"

Brett dismounted and handed the reins to the boy.
"These four. I'm staying at the hotel. Do you sleep in
the barn?"

"Sure do. Got my bed and stuff in the tack room at
the other end."

"That's good. I don't know how long we'll be in
Abilene or when we'll be leaving. Could be at any time
of the day or night. I'll pay for any inconvenience."

"Thanks, sir. Much appreciated."

"Good sized place you have here. Expecting an
increase in business?"

"Yes, sir. The boss expects a lot of new business in
the next few years." He raised an arm in leaving and led
the horses toward the corral.

Brett called after him, "Where are they going to
build the shipping pens and the railroad station?"

The boy stopped. He looked a bit perplexed. "Right
over there." He pointed beyond the livery barn. "Least,
that's what they say. Never saw a train, but I bet it'll
scare the horses."

"They'll get used to the noise after a while."

The boy frowned, turned and walked toward the corral.

Brett went back to the street and down the dusty middle toward the hotel. The street was deserted. Not a soul in sight. He stepped up on the boardwalk and went in.

No one stood at the desk. He was surprised to see the key to his room hanging on the keyboard. *I should have reminded her to lock the door. I don't trust anybody, especially drunk cowboys.* He hurried around the counter, took the room key and sprinted up the stairs, three steps at a time.

He tried the knob of the bedroom door. It was unlocked. He opened the door slowly, partially. He saw Winona standing in the corner, looking at him. Her face was blank, showing neither fear nor surprise. Pushing the door open, he saw the cowboy on his back on the bed. His belt was loosened, and his pants unbuttoned. His shirt was soaked with blood from the knife in his chest.

Brett leaned back through the door and looked back down the hall. Seeing no one, he closed the door slowly. He went to Winona, put his arms around her shoulders, and held her. "I'm sorry," he said. "I meant to tell you to get the key and lock the door, but I forgot. I'm sorry." He leaned back. "Are you okay?"

"I okay. *He* not okay." She motioned with her head toward the body. "What we do?"

He stared at the window. *This is going to be dicey.* He pulled the knife slowly from the cowboy's chest, wiped the blade on the body's shirt. He handed the knife to Winona. "Where do you keep it?"

She picked up the leather scabbard from the floor, showed it to him, and pushed the knife in it. She dropped the scabbard on a pannier in the corner.

He looked around the room, stared at the window, pondering. He spoke softly. "We're going to put him under the bed. There's no blood on the bedspread, and we need to keep it that way. Help me lift him off the bed to the floor."

Pulling the body to the edge of the bed, he lifted the shoulders while she took the legs. They lifted and lowered the body to the floor. He pushed it under the bed edge, then went around the bed to the other side, crawled under and pulled the body full under the bed where it could not be seen by anyone standing in the room.

He scooted from under the bed and stood. "Help me make the bed." They straightened covers and smoothed the bedspread. "We're going now. I wish we could leave after dark, but his pards will be looking for him. They probably knew where he was going when he left the saloon. When we go outside, we'll walk to the right so we won't pass the saloon, then go behind the row of stores to reach the livery. Understand that?" She nodded.

Brett tied the saddlebag, threw it over his shoulder, hefted the panniers, and stepped toward the door. He stopped abruptly, slid the saddlebag from his shoulder onto the bed. Untying the flap, he reached into the bag and pulled out the wallet. He took out some bills, replaced the wallet in the bag and closed the flap.

He picked up the panniers and reached for the saddlebag. Winona already had it on her shoulder. She pointed at the door.

Brett opened the door, looked down the hall. Seeing no one, he stepped out. Winona followed. He closed the door and locked it. They walked down the hall and down the stairs to the lobby. There was no clerk, nor anyone else. Brett put the bills and room key on the shelf below the counter.

Passing through the front door, they looked in both directions. Three women walked on the boardwalk across the street from the saloon, chatting and laughing. Two men stood at the hitching rail a few storefronts down on the other side of the street. They gestured as they talked, one pointing down the street in the other direction. Two men stood at the hitching rail in front of the saloon. One had a hand on his horse's hindquarters as he spoke with his companion.

"They same men, I think," Winona said softly.

"Yes, I think so. Can't be helped. Maybe they won't notice us." He stepped off the walk into the street, and she followed. They walked to the right, away from the saloon. At the end of the row of storefronts, just before reaching the side of the last building, he turned to see the two men looking over the backs of their horses, staring directly at them.

They walked to the building on the end, a clothing store. A man in a suit and tie stood at the open door. He smiled and started to speak, but they passed and he watched them disappear around the corner of the shop.

At the side of the building, Brett paused, took Winona's arm and stopped her. Pondering, he stared into space. He looked back toward the road, leaned to her and spoke softly. She nodded and walked around the building to the back.

She walked through the scattered debris common to

backyards anywhere. She passed the first building and then the second. Approaching the passageway between the second and third buildings, she stopped abruptly. Two men stepped from the passageway into her path. It was the two men from the saloon, pards of the cowboy who now lay dead under the hotel bed.

"Well, well, well, what we got here," said the cowboy. He grinned.

His companion did not. "Where is he, you damn whore? We know he went lookin' for yah. He watched the two of you and knew where you was goin'. You musta seen him. Where is he!" He stepped toward her. She backed away.

"That'll do, boys." The two spun around and saw Brett, his pistol leveled on them. He had stepped from a passageway between two buildings.

The two cowboys were speechless a moment. The belligerent one finally recovered and spoke. "We don't want no trouble, man. We're just looking for Eddie. He had a snootful and went looking for the woman."

"If he had a snootful, he's probably passed out and is sleeping it off. You'll need to look for him."

"Th' hell you say! I know you had to've seen 'im! He was after your whore and left the saloon right after you did!" He stepped toward Brett.

Brett brought the six-shooter up a foot from his face. He spoke softly. "One more step, and I'll blow a hole in your head, you son-of-a-bitch."

"C'mon, Freddie," his pard said, looking nervously at Brett. "Let's look for him. Abilene ain't that big. We'll find him."

"That's good advice, Freddie," said Brett. He pushed the muzzle of his pistol into Freddie's cheek.

Freddie stepped back, frowning at Brett. He threw a quick glance at Winona who stared blankly at him.

Freddie took his companion by the arm, and they stumbled down the passageway between shops toward the road.

Brett watched the men until they rounded the front of the building and disappeared. He took Winona's arm and stepped off. "Now we gotta hurry. They may look for him, or they may get their guns and a few friends and come looking for us. Chances are they saw him go into the hotel and will soon find what's left of him."

At the livery, Brett awoke the napping hand, paid him, and asked him to help saddle and bridle the horses and tie on the panniers. The hand stared open-mouthed at the bills.

Brett and Winona mounted quickly and set out at a lope in a northeasterly direction across the prairie. Brett looked back anxiously and saw no activity at the livery. They rode over a rising and down into a shallow arroyo, continued riding in a slow lope.

After another ten minutes, they pulled up. Brett dismounted, pulled the binocular from the saddlebag and climbed up the slope of the arroyo. He focused on the back trail. *There they are!* Two riders at a lope followed the direction they had taken from the livery. He slid down the slope hurriedly, stowed the binocular, and mounted.

"Changing direction." He kicked his horse to a gallop due west, Winona following. They took care to remain out of sight, in the arroyo and behind a rising, for fifteen minutes before climbing out and riding at a gallop westward.

―――――――

Dusk. The sun had just dropped below the horizon, and the lacy clouds above the sunset were a riot of soft colors. They sat at a campfire, the low flames flickering and popping from the bones and fatty tissue of a prairie chicken they dropped into the fire after cleaning the bones. Winona had roasted the chicken on a pointed stick leaning over the fire.

Winona licked her fingers and rubbed her hands on grass. "I like chicken."

"Yes, I thought you did since I had to almost fight you for a share of it."

She smiled, leaned over, and kissed him on the cheek. "I glad white men teach Cheyenne to kiss. I like kisses." She pulled his face around and kissed his lips.

He put a hand behind her head and kissed her hard on the mouth. "Mmm. I'm glad, too." He released her, picked up a stick and stirred the fire, sending up sparks. He tossed the stick on the flames. The stick caught and small flames erupted from it, died, and became part of the bed of glowing embers.

He stared at the embers. "Didn't know you had a knife."

She looked aside at him, back to the fire. "Sarah give to me. You remember Sarah, white woman I lived with?" He nodded. "She give to me before we left house to run away from her husband. She said white men can be bad, and I might need it."

He picked up a stick behind him and stirred the embers. "Why haven't you told me about it?"

"I... I didn't know..." She looked at him, then looked down at her hands in her lap.

He took her hand. "It's okay. You had no way of knowing whether I was going to hurt you."

She took his hand in both of hers. "That was true when we met, when we were together at village and fort. But I know now you are good man." She looked down. "I forgot about knife. I should have told you. I sorry."

He put an arm around her shoulders and pulled her to him. "Sweetheart, you have nothing to apologize for. I can't begin to know how you feel about what is happening to you and to your people. I wish... I wish I could do something." He squeezed his eyes tightly shut, shook his head violently.

Sweetheart. The worst is yet to come. If there were only something I could do. I know what's happening, I know what's going to happen, and I can do nothing. Nothing! If there is a God in heaven, if you are a loving God, why are you letting this happen to these people? Why?

She touched his cheek and wiped his tears. "I sorry. Are you okay, honey?"

He kissed her lips, held her. "As long as I can hold you like this, I'm okay. Let's get to bed. We have some decisions to make tomorrow."

He went to the horses he had hobbled nearby in a patch of grass. Bending beside his mount, he checked the hobbles. He straightened, flexed his back, looked up into a clear gray sky, stars popping out as darkness deepened. The silence was broken by the soft howl of a coyote in the distance, a sound he had come to love, mournful and longing. He went to the packhorses, untied panniers and pulled out blankets.

She took the blankets and rolled them out beside

the fire while he dropped an armload of dry sticks on the flames.

They pulled off boots, lay on the blanket, and pulled up the cover. Brett sat up, took off his pistol belt and laid it beside the saddle, his makeshift pillow.

He leaned over, kissed her cheek. She reached under the cover to touch him and heard his heavy breathing. She smiled to herself, rolled onto her back.

She stared into the clear dark sky, stars popping, twinkling. In the distance, the haunting howl of a wolf.

Suddenly her eyes opened wide at snuffling on the other side of the fire circle. Their horses were hobbled behind them on this side of the fire. She rolled over to whisper in Brett's ear. "Honey Brett. I hear something, a horse, I think, not ours."

He was awake immediately and reached quietly for his holster. Pushing the blanket down slowly, he rolled on his side, withdrawing the pistol as he raised on his knees. Looking in the direction of the snuffling, he stood without a sound, knowing that he was dimly illuminated by the glow from the firepit.

He stepped away from the fire, away from Winona. More snuffling and a shifting by their horses. He leaned forward, straining, made out a shadow, dimly outlined by the glow from the firepit.

Brett leveled his six-shooter at the specter. "Show yourself!" he shouted.

He flinched at a shot from the darkness. He fired at the muzzle flash, then fired again, and again. At the same time, another shot sounded.

He ran to the fire, saw Winona standing there, holding the rifle. He bent and grasped the dry end of a burning limb. "Stay here," he said softly to Winona. He held the stick high for illumination, walked into the darkness, pistol pointed ahead, and saw the two bodies. They lay beside a prostrate horse that gurgled, wide-eyed, head raised off the ground as it struggled to rise.

He nudged each body with a boot, and both were still. He went to the horse. "Sorry, old man." He shot the horse in the eye. The head jerked up, fell heavily to the ground and was still. He stroked the horse's neck.

He walked to the fire, bent and pushed the pistol into the holster. He took the rifle from Winona, laid it over a saddle and took her in his arms. "Okay?" he said. She nodded, her head against his chest. "Forgot I had taken the Henry from my horse before hobbling. Sure glad I did.

"Winnie, there are two dead men out there. I'm sure it's the two from Abilene. I don't care a whit about them, but we killed a horse, too. I feel bad about that. The other horse must be halfway to Abilene by now.

"We're moving camp. I don't want to be anywhere near that pair when they are found. We have a clear sky and good moonlight, and we'll take it slow."

They saddled and bridled the horses, checked the panniers on the packhorses, removed hobbles and set out, slowly, carefully. The land was softly illuminated by the bright moon, and they made their way slowly.

CHAPTER 6

Brett opened his eyes and looked up into a cloudless deep blue sky. He pushed the blanket down, sat up, and looked around. The grassy slope from the campground stretched below, empty and dry, to the distant horizon. He had selected the camping spot in soft moonlight and decided this morning he had made a good choice. There was no snow in sight. Indeed, a light breeze, almost warm, touched his cheek. For some reason that he could not have explained to himself, he felt good this morning.

He leaned over and kissed Winona on a cheek. He caressed a breast and kissed her neck. She grunted, pushed him and rolled away from him. He kissed her nape.

"Stop that! Go to bushes or something." She snuggled and pulled the blanket up.

Patting the top of her head, he pulled the blanket around her shoulder and sat up. He rubbed his face vigorously with both hands then pulled on his boots. Standing, he looked up at the flute-like call of an unseen meadowlark. He scanned the prairie below the camp and saw no movement.

He frowned, trying to remember last night, selecting this site in near darkness. It looked like a good spot last night, but something bothered him now. *What am I missing?*

He shrugged, walked into a dense stand of chokecherry to relieve himself. He smiled at the memory a few days ago when he absentmindedly peed in full view of Winona. "I don't like see that," she had said. "Go someplace." After that, he had always found bushes or a rocky hiding place.

Buttoning his pants, he walked through the chokecherry thicket to the other side. Emerging from the bushes, he stopped abruptly.

What th' hell!

Instead of the rolling grassy prairie where they had camped last evening, he looked down a steep rocky slope to a distant line of pine and spruce, suggesting a stream.

What th' hell!

He squinted. In the dark mass under the trees, which he thought were shadows, he sensed movement. He tensed suddenly.

Winnie!

He crashed back through the chokecherry and knelt beside the blankets. He pulled the blanket down and saw her. She rolled over, saw him through sleepy eyes, pulled the blanket back to her chin, frowned at him.

"You—" Then she saw his expression. She pushed the blanket down and sat up quickly. "What is it? Something wrong?"

He took her in his arms. "I was afraid I might have lost you."

"Brett, honey, you no make sense. What do you mean?"

He stood. "I'll explain. No time now. Get ready. We may have to leave in a hurry." He went quickly around the fire circle to his saddle on the ground near the hobbled horses. He opened his saddlebag and pulled out the binocular.

Winona sat on the blankets, watching him.

He moved into the thicket and stopped just before emerging, staying hidden. He trained the binocular on the line of trees. He straightened, straining.

He moved the binocular along the line of trees and the tents beneath them. He saw soldiers standing at fire circles and wandering about. Then he saw the flags.

My god! It can't be! Not again.

His jaw dropped, and he felt dizzy, almost losing the binocular. He scoured his memory and suddenly was sure. He was looking at the swallowtail guidon of alternating red and white horizontal stripes and a circle of white stars on a blue field, the flag carried by the United States Seventh Cavalry. He moved the binocular and focused on the second flag, a swallowtail of red and blue horizontal fields with two crossed white sabers in the center. He lowered the binocular, squeezed his eyes shut, then opened them and looked again through the binocular.

After a moment, he lowered the binocular slowly. This was the personal headquarters flag of Lieutenant Colonel George Armstrong Custer.

He stared at the line of trees and tents. His mind raced. *Custer? Bizarre. Where in hell are we? Is this*

*training maneuvers? An action during the Civil War?
Custer was a successful Civil War leader. Or something
in the West? The countryside looks more western than
southern. If western, then...*

He squinted, his face contorted, as he tried to
remember. *Think! Dammit, think!* Custer led a force of
a thousand men of the Seventh Cavalry into the Black
Hills in July of 1874, in violation of the 1868 Treaty of
Fort Laramie which set the region aside for the exclu-
sive use of the Sioux. Custer's orders were to look for a
location for a fort and to investigate the rumor of gold in
the region. *Could this be that expedition? Yet...the
country doesn't look like the pictures I've seen of the
Black Hills.*

*On the other hand... my god! The other famous
campaign of Custer in the West. This country looks
more like southeastern Montana where the Battle of the
Little Bighorn was fought. I've seen pictures. I'm going
mad. I swear it.*

Binocular in hand, he pushed back through the
chokecherry brambles. "Winnie, we need—"

"Brett," she said, softly. Brett stopped. Three
mounted soldiers sat their horses beside the campfire,
their pistols trained on Winona. One of the soldiers
moved his pistol slowly to point at Brett.

Brett frowned, his mind racing. "Hello, boys," he
said. "Are you with the column below?"

"Yeah," said the corporal who leveled on Brett.
"Who you with? Who are you, out here by yourself
with a Indian woman?"

Brett squared his jaw, stared at the soldier,
pondered. He felt his brain ready to explode. *What
the hell. Why not?* "I'm a newspaperman. *Chicago*

Courier sent me to cover the Seventh Cav. My bosses know that Colonel Custer welcomes newspaper coverage of his campaigns." Winona stared blankly at Brett.

The soldiers looked at each other. They lowered their pistols, pushed them into holsters. The corporal who had done the talking pursed his lips, looked aside, frowned. "You're going with us."

Brett nodded to Winona. She gathered up the blankets and stuffed them and cooking gear into the packhorse panniers while Brett slowly bridled and saddled the horses and worked on the hobbles. Slowly. *I need time to think.* This done, he and Winona mounted and followed the corporal, the other two riding behind the packhorses.

During the ride down the slope toward the army encampment, Brett's mind boiled as he tried to dredge up everything he knew about Custer and the campaign. *If I could only Google the Great Sioux War, I would have all I need!* He almost smiled, shook his head at the absurdity.

"Honey?"

He looked aside at Winona. "It's okay," he said softly. "I'll explain later."

———

"Tell me," Winona said.

They sat at a small fire at the middle of the large army encampment of tents and rope corrals. The corporal who had led them to the camp had reported to his lieutenant who assigned them a small tent. Soldiers ambled by, chatting, glancing their way, eying Winona, commenting and chuckling softly. Brett stared them down, but they took no notice.

Brett exhaled deeply, looked up at the tree canopy, softly illuminated at dusk by many campfires. "I have told you how I came to be at Sand Creek. From the year 2022 to your time, 1864. Now, unless I am completely mad, and that's a real possibility, we have been transported to Montana in the year 1876. Winnie, the most astonishing thing about all this is that you were transported with me. I can't tell you why or how. I don't understand why I am here, and I know even less why you are here with me. But I'm so relieved."

"What is happening? Why are all the soldiers here? What are they doing here?"

He looked up again at the canopy, then to Winona. "I am cursed, Winnie. I know what is going to happen, and I can do nothing to change it. Maybe I am a shaman, after all. Or a demon of some sort."

She took his hand. "You didn't decide to be what you are, and you didn't decide to be where you are. Tell me what is happening."

He looked into the fire. "The last few years have been very bad for the Sioux and other tribes around here, especially Northern Cheyenne and Arapaho. The government had agreed that the tribes had a right to their ancestral lands. But when gold was discovered on those lands, and whites wanted to settle on those lands, the army was called in to protect the whites. This led to many battles.

"It's not over. This army here will soon meet a large force of Sioux, Cheyenne, and Arapaho. There will be a big battle." He looked around, leaned toward her, spoke softly. "Winnie, the tribes will win."

Her eyes opened wide. "That is good, that is so good."

He sobered, fed the fire from the pile of dry sticks at his side. The night at mid-June had turned cool, and he shivered, partly from the weather, partly from what he knew of the approaching conflict and aftermath of the Battle of the Little Bighorn.

———

Next morning, Brett had just begun to build a fire, on his knees at the fire circle, when a soldier, carrying two plates of beans, biscuits, and potatoes, stopped when he saw Winona crawl from the tent. She stood and walked to the fire circle, running fingers through her long hair. She walked slowly to Brett, looking at the soldier, her face blank.

The soldier gaped, his jaw hanging, holding the plates before him. She wore her buckskin dress and was barefoot. Since he would pass her off as his interpreter, Brett thought it wise that she looked Indian rather than a native woman in the man's clothes Brett had bought from the Santa Fé trader.

Brett took the plates. "Thank you. Will you be doing this again, or will we be joining you and the others at meals?"

"Oh, I'll be bringing plates to you." He responded to Brett, but stared at Winona.

"That's very kind of you. I'm Brett, this is Winona. What's your name, corporal?"

"Jimmy. Just Jimmy." He smiled, almost bowing.

"Thank you, Jimmy," Winona said softly to the soldier.

"Yes, ma'am," he mumbled. He stood a moment longer, then turned abruptly and strode toward a knot of soldiers who had watched Jimmy from the time he approached Bret and Winona.

When the soldier came up to them, they laughed, jostling him. "Ma'am?" said one of the soldiers. Jimmy smiled and walked away with them, all still joking and back-slapping.

Brett watched all this, sober. He turned to Winona. "Now the whole army will know that there is an Indian woman in camp who is young, pretty, and speaks good English. We'll need to be careful."

They were still eating breakfast when a lieutenant walked up. "The Colonel wants to see you. Come with me, please." His eyes darted between Brett and Winona while he spoke, eventually resting on Brett. Brett nodded, set his plate on the ground, stood and offered a hand to Winona. She ignored the hand, put her plate on his and stood, brushing off her dress. The lieutenant set out, looked back to see them following.

They stopped at the large tent where Custer's swallowtail flag was planted in front. The lieutenant stepped inside, disappearing from view. "I have the strangers, Colonel."

Brett inhaled deeply, cleared his throat nervously, leaned toward Winona and whispered, "Here we go again." He took her hand, squeezed it lightly, and released it.

The lieutenant appeared at the tent entrance and extended a hand inside. Brett and Winona walked in. Though he knew what to expect, Brett was stunned to stand before Custer in the flesh. He sat at a table, dressed in his distinctive fringed buckskin coat, unsmiling and seemingly detached or bored. He did not offer them the chairs beside the table. Brett nodded to the stocky lieutenant with long side whiskers standing behind Custer. *That would be Lieutenant Cooke, Custer's adjutant.*

"I'm told you are a correspondent," Custer said.

"Yes, sir. *Chicago Tribune." Courier, damn it, Courier.* "My readers will be most interested to read about your campaign."

Custer frowned. "And what campaign is that? What do you know about our mission here?"

"Very little. Only that there has been unrest in the region since the events in the Black Hills."

"Events" indeed! Custer led the Seventh Cav into the Black Hills two years before, in 1874, to select a location for a fort while civilians searched for gold. A rush to the region followed though the Sioux had been promised in treaties that the land would be guaranteed to them. The Sioux called the whites who soon occupied the land "thieves" and Custer, "chief of all thieves".

"Hmm. Well, I do think the people have a right to know what the army does to protect our citizens and their best interests. Just keep a low profile. General Sherman does not agree with me on what we're doing here. Keep that in mind when you write your pieces."

Custer looked at Winona. "I'm told this woman is your interpreter?"

"Yes, sir. Winona is Cheyenne. She also speaks Arapahoe, Sioux, and English."

"Perhaps she should be on my staff." Custer had not taken his eyes from her.

Brett responded quickly, a bit sharply. "We're at your service, Colonel. If you should need our assistance, we are happy to oblige." He assumed that his emphasis on "we" made it clear that he would entertain no call for Winona's giving any assistance without his presence.

Custer stood. "We move out... well, soon," Custer said. "Ride close behind me, not with me, but close, in case I wish to speak to you." He looked at Winona. "Or your interpreter."

"Thank you, sir," said Brett, "we'll do that." He and Winona walked from the tent. He nodded to the lieutenant who had summoned them, and they went to their campsite.

Standing at the fire circle, Brett frowned, looked down at the ashes, then to her. "Winnie, I just remembered something. I recall from a book about this campaign that Custer in fact had a newspaperman with the army."

Winona smiled. "You wonder if the newspaper man in the book is *you*."

Brett pursed his lips. "Well? I'll have to read the accounts of this campaign again." He looked aside. "If I ever have a chance to read the Custer accounts. Or the accounts of Sand Creek. Or Bent's new fort. Or the post-war Santa Fé trade. Or Abilene." He rubbed his face hard with both hands, lowered his hands and turned to Winona. His eyes misted.

She took him in her arms. "It's going be okay, honey sweetheart." She held him, and he hugged her, resting his head on hers.

He spoke softly. "Winnie, if some morning I fail to wake up, or if you don't see me in my bed, you'll know I have gone away, transported somewhere, and you shouldn't worry."

"Don't say that," she said softly. "I don't want think about that."

————

That night, lying wide awake in his bed, he stared at the dark peak of the tent. *I'm afraid to sleep. I'm afraid I'll lose her. What will happen to me if I'm transported, and she's not with me?"* He reached over, touched her arm. She stirred, pulled the blanket to her chin, exhaled heavily.

He rolled over on his back. *How can I ever sleep again?* He remembered the verse his mother taught him as a child.

> *Now I lay me down to sleep*
> *I pray the Lord my soul to keep*
> *If I should die before I wake*
> *I pray the Lord my soul to take.*

Does God read history? Or fantasy? Whoever or whatever controls my destiny, please give me another day with Winnie. He rolled over till his body touched hers, his head lightly against hers. He closed his eyes, the tension melted away, and he slept.

————

Next morning, he and Winona had just come out from their tent when Jimmy appeared, smiling broadly, holding their breakfast plates on a tray with one hand and two coffee cups in the other.

"Look at this, Winnie! Early breakfast and coffee!"

"Didn't know if you drank coffee, miss—"

"Winnie," she said.

He nodded, smiling, "Uh, Winnie. And Brett."

Brett took the tray as Winnie accepted the proffered cups. "Thank you, Jimmy," she said. "I drink coffee sometimes."

Jimmy smiled, nodded a couple of times, spun around and walked briskly away, chin up.

Winona and Brett looked at each other. "He a good man, Jimmy," Winona said.

"Boy, more likely. Couldn't be more'n eighteen or nineteen. Probably joined the army for some adventure or just for a job."

They sat at their cold fire circle and ate in silence. When he had finished his plate and drained his cup, he turned to her. "You gonna drink that coffee?" She had tasted it, but screwed up her face and set it down. She handed the cup to him. When they had finished, they set the plates and cups on the ground at the fire pit for Jimmy to collect.

As Winona prepared for moving camp, Brett wandered among soldiers busily breaking camp and making ready for the day's march. He listened to their talk about the progress and problems of the campaign. It seemed the excitement about the prospect of battle with the savages was muted lately by a growing awareness of the size of the enemy forces.

Scouts had found the remains of vast encampments of lodges and wickiups, only recently abandoned. On an afternoon scout, Brett rode with the Ree scouts, favored by Custer, who saw the scalp of a white man hanging from a frame. The Rees muttered softly among themselves, their demeanor betraying fear of something.

Beyond the encampments, scouts saw broad trails where the grass was eaten for miles, the land scattered with the droppings of thousands of horses. On one stretch, the dust was six inches deep, the trail half a mile wide. All of the trails invariably were marked by dragging lodgepoles. Everyone in the army camp, old campaigners and fuzzy-cheeked recruits alike, knew by now that thousands of Indians were converging for the annual summer sun dance. The old-timers opined that this meant 3,500 to 4,000 warriors would be in the throng.

Added to the growing concern about the size of the enemy force, there was an ominous portent. On the march one day, during a stop, Custer's personal swallowtail flag blew down to the rear. Captain Godfrey picked it up and planted it. It blew down a second time, again to the rear. Godfrey replanted the swallowtail, only to see it sagging in a stiff breeze. The double fall backward and the limp cloth in a breeze was seen by many as a bad omen, a prediction of defeat. When he was told about it, Custer was unmoved.

Brett could only shake his head when he heard about the incident. He had never seen it in the accounts of the Little Bighorn.

———

Early one morning, Brett and Winona rode with some Crow scouts who were searching the countryside ahead and left of the column's route. Winona did not speak Crow, but one of the scouts knew some Sioux, enough that they could communicate.

After they had ridden a few miles, Winona told Brett that she needed to stop to relieve herself.

"Tell them we'll catch up," said Brett. She spoke to the Crow who understood Sioux. He nodded and said something. She smiled, held up a hand, replied sharply. He spoke to the other scouts, and they rode ahead.

"What was that all about?" said Brett.

"He said he would help. I told him go away." She and Brett rode into a pine copse, dismounted, and tied their reins to a low serviceberry bush. She disappeared behind a boulder.

"Can I help?" he said.

"No! You stay there."

"Hurry up. We should find the scouts or get back to the column." He went to the tethered horses. Suddenly a distant shot sounded, and the bullet ricocheted from the boulder that sheltered Winona. "Down!" He ran to stand behind a large tree trunk.

"Winnie, tell them we are friends and stop shooting."

Winona moved to the side of the boulder and shouted in Cheyenne in the direction of the shot. Three shots peppered the foliage and boulder. She shouted again, this time in Sioux, with the same result. They winced at the sound of the bullets striking around them. She leaned out from her cover and yelled in Arapahoe, then jerked back when shots followed.

"Stop shooting, stop!" she shouted in English.

Silence. Then, a shout from the distance. "Who's there?"

"We're with the column!" Brett yelled. "Brett and Winona!"

Silence. Then: "Okay. Come out so we can see you."

Winona peered from behind the boulder at Brett. He nodded, stepped from behind his cover and slowly walked a few steps from the copse. Winona moved up beside him.

They saw five soldiers stand and step from behind cover.

"We're mounting and will ride to you. Okay?" shouted Brett.

"Come on," from the soldiers.

Winona and Brett mounted and rode across the grassy flat to the soldiers who were in the process of mounting.

"You're gonna get yourselves shot, talking in Indian," said one of the soldiers.

"We thought you were Indians scouting the army," Brett said.

Brett and Winona fell in behind the soldiers and rode with them to the army column a few miles distant.

————

Brett and Winona lay in their bed, breathing heavily, evenly. She wiped his forehead with a hand. He kissed her lips, rolled over on his back and exhaled deeply.

She put a finger to his lips. "You need be more quiet," she said softly. "You sound like bull moose look for girl moose."

"Me? You sound like a screeching train whistle."

"Shhh. People hear." She rolled over to face him, reached her arm across his chest. "I never hear train whistle."

"Just listen to yourself next time." He kissed her lips.

They were still, quiet. Winona pulled up the blanket, snuggled against his shoulder. After a long moment, he rolled over to face her.

He spoke softly, almost a whisper. "Winnie, I think we should go to the Indian camp. I know what is going to happen in all this, and I don't want to watch what is going to happen from the army camp." *If we stay with the army, we'll be watching people die. I know I will survive. But Winnie?*

"There's nothing we can do here. There's nothing I could say that would influence Custer. The ass is bent on using this battle to send him to the White House. He wants to be President of the United States.

"If we were in the Indian camp, I can't change the outcome, but we might be able to save some lives and maybe even influence what comes later. The histories I have read don't tell everything that happened. What do you think?"

"Yes. We go."

————

The bugle shattered the silence at dawn. It was the first bugle call in days. The army broke camp rapidly and moved out in quick time.

Brett sensed that battle with the Indians was near, if not today, then tomorrow almost surely. He knew they must act now, but they had to take care since the officers would be on edge this morning. Some were still unsure, perhaps a bit suspicious, of this white man and his Indian woman.

Brett and Winona moved in slow motion. They took the tent down methodically, folded it up carefully, dallied with their blankets, rubbed down the horses, saddled their mounts, carefully, slowly. All this while the column moved in good order past them, soldiers glancing their way, then urging their horses to keep up.

Brett and Winona had seen the order of march on previous days and now watched it move by. First were the scouts, white plainsmen and Indians—Arikiras, Rees, and Crows. There also was the newspaperman, Mark Kellogg, on his mule. Brett had overhead the name and remembered him from a history he had read. Brett waved and Kellogg returned the wave, frowning. Perhaps someone had told him about this other newsman.

Next came the long column of soldiers, two by two, followed by a small herd of extra horses and the straggling line of pack mules, herded by sweating, cursing soldiers.

Brett and Winona stood idly beside their saddled mounts, fussing with stirrups and cinches. They watched the column moving ahead, finally disappearing behind a rising, sounds of creaking leather and occasional shouts growing dim.

"Now," said Brett. He pushed the folded tent and loaded panniers into dense bushes at streamside, out of sight. Winona meanwhile removed halters from the unburdened packhorses and slapped rumps. The horses shied and trotted aside. Untying reins, Brett and Winona quickly mounted and waded across the shallow creek and up the opposite bank. Once on top, they kicked their horses into a gallop across a flat, away from the column and toward the assumed location of the Indian encampment.

———

Brett and Winona sat their horses in shadow at the edge of a stand of pines. Brett held the binocular with both hands, looking across a broad meadow at a line of trees.

"Do you see anything?" she said.

"Yeah. Trees."

"I see something move. Look under the two tall trees together."

He moved the binocular, lowered it, and looked at her. "How in—"

"You see it now?"

He looked again through the binocular. "Yeah, I see it. Don't know how in hell you saw it. Can't tell if it's animals or... it's people! Here, you look." He handed her the binocular. He had practiced use of the binocular with her only last week. She took it and looked at the woods.

"People. Many Indian people," she said, handing him the binocular. "We go there."

"What! They will shoot us down before we ride ten yards."

She touched her horse's belly and rode slowly from the shade into sunlight.

"Winnie! You'll get us killed!"

She shouted loudly in Cheyenne toward the distant wood, then in Sioux, waving an arm, still walking her horse. Brett urged his mount up beside her.

She shouted again, waved an arm. Two riders emerged from the wood ahead, walked into the open.

She shouted again. Three more riders appeared from the wood, all watching the two strangers coming.

I can't believe I'm doing this. We're not going to reach those woods except as corpses.

She shouted again. More riders emerged from the wood, watching. *Probably wondering who in hell would be so dumb to ride to their deaths yelling their heads off, at least one of them.* He looked at Winona. She was smiling.

A shout came from the Indians. Winona kicked her mount to a fast lope. Brett shook his head and followed. By the time they arrived at the group of warriors, half a dozen others had ridden from the woods.

Winona and Brett pulled up in front of the group. There followed a rapid exchange in Cheyenne between Winona and the Indian who seemed to be the leader of the group. Brett could understand little, but knew enough to realize it was Cheyenne rather than other languages Winona knew. The Indian spoke sharply, angrily it seemed, shaking a fist at Brett and waving a rifle over his head. A couple of warriors behind him also brandished rifles.

Winona replied in a strong, confident voice, gesturing toward Brett without looking at him. The Indian leader seemed to relax and responded in a softer voice, and others sitting their horses near him laughed. She looked at Brett, smiling.

A warrior who sat his horse at the back of the group moved to the front, holding a rifle over his head. He shouted, lowered the rifle, and leveled on Brett.

Winona spoke loudly, pointing at Brett. The leader quickly moved his horse in front of the warrior with the gun, pushing the barrel aside. He turned to Winona, frowning, spoke softly. The others were quiet, listening. She replied, looking back and forth between the leader and Brett.

The group was silent, stunned it seemed, staring at Brett. After a long moment, the leader said something sharply to Winona, wheeled his horse and moved off at a gallop, followed by the others, a dozen in all. Winona started to follow.

"Winnie, wait. What was that all about? I thought they were going to shoot us, me at least."

She laughed. "They very angry at whites. Some want shoot you. I say you good man, friend of Indians, and you want help Indians. Some say they might shoot you anyway, just because you wrong color. That when some laugh."

"The one with the rifle at the end wasn't laughing. The leader saved me. Why? What did you say?"

She lowered her head, hesitated, reached up to rub her horse's neck. "I thought he going shoot you. I say... I say you have strong medicine. Sometimes you can see ahead, see what is going to happen." She reached over and touched his arm. "I sorry. I not know what to do. I think he going to kill you."

He frowned. "Hmm. Well, this could be a problem." He smiled faintly and looked at her. "At least, I'm alive to deal with it. Don't be sorry. Your quick wit saved my life." He reached over, took an arm, pulled her to him, and kissed her on the cheek. "What did he say as they were leaving?"

"He say we come with them to village."

———

Brett and Winona sat their horses with the Indians on a bluff overlooking the largest Indian village Brett had ever seen in books or imagined. He was stunned. Lodges below were crowded close and extended for hundreds of yards in all directions, disappearing around a turn in the stream. He recalled reading that there were three thousand lodges in the gathering, housing 8,000 to 10,000 people, and perhaps 3,500 to 4,000 warriors. Further, as many as 1,000 warriors had left Sioux government agencies in Nebraska recently to join the force here.

Custer, Custer, Custer. You egotistical, pompous, stupid ass. Even if I told you what's going to happen to you and your command, you would not believe me and would probably have me shot as a dangerous madman.

CHAPTER 7

The Indians rode down a winding trail from the bluff to the village below. As they rode among the lodges, women stopped their cooking and mending at the strange spectacle of a white man and an Indian woman riding with their men. The women whispered among themselves, some speaking to the warriors as they passed. The riders replied briefly to them or ignored them.

The leader reined up before a lodge and spoke to Winona. He gestured to the lodge and Winona responded, nodding. The warriors rode on. When Winona did not follow, Brett frowned.

"He say we stay here," she said. "He talk to chiefs and come back. He say keep horses here. Maybe we not gonna stay here."

While Brett unsaddled the horses and hobbled them in sparse grass behind the lodge, Winona untied the blankets from behind saddles and carried them inside. This done, they stood together before the lodge, only then aware that everyone in sight was staring at them. Women soon returned to their work at fire circles or sitting before lodges, minding children and chatting, glancing often at the two strangers.

Brett found a stick behind the lodge and worked on digging a shallow fire pit while Winona gathered small stones for the circle. He stood, scratched his head. "I hope we have some use for the pit besides warming ourselves. We don't have any stores of any kind." He looked around. "Maybe somebody will invite us to supper."

Dumping her armload of stones at the rough pit, she knelt and arranged them in a circle. She stood, looking down the passage between lodges. Dusting her hands, she rubbed them on her dress. "I don't think we go hungry." She motioned with a nod toward the warrior approaching. It was the leader of the bunch that had brought them to the camp.

The warrior spoke with Winona, ignoring Brett. He turned and strode back the way he had come. Winona followed, beckoning to Brett. He lagged, frowning, his mind racing, as he tried to recount the conflict that would culminate in the upcoming Battle of the Little Bighorn.

Sioux and Northern Cheyenne in 1873 fought railroad survey parties and the army when they entered hunting grounds in eastern Montana guaranteed to the tribes by the Treaty of Fort Laramie. The army force was led by Custer. The following year, Custer was ordered to the Black Hills in western Dakota Territory to investigate rumors of gold deposits. This action also was seen by the tribes as a violation of the Fort Laramie treaty. Custer confirmed the presence of large gold deposits, and this set off a rush of prospectors to the region.

The Indians protested this invasion of their lands, but the gleam of gold, not the clauses in a treaty, decided the issue. Thousands of miners flooded the hills, increasing the pressure on Washington. Government eventually decreed that all Sioux must move peacefully to a reservation in Dakota by January 1876, or the army would force the move.

When the Sioux did not comply, the western army, under Generals Sherman and Sheridan, acted. Beginning in March 1876 and continuing for a year and a half, a series of expeditions, large and small, were launched against the tribes.

The first expedition actually was conducted against the Northern Cheyenne, not the Sioux. The Cheyenne were outraged and joined forces with the Sioux to fight the army. News of the fighting reached the Sioux agencies in Dakota and Nebraska, and many of the men living there left the agencies to join the fight.

Custer's march on the Indian encampment at the Little Bighorn was part of this campaign against the Sioux and Cheyenne. It was the culmination of the campaign, though no army brass or Indian leader would know this. Only Brett knew it.

As they walked through the village, though he knew something of the force that Custer was about to encounter, he was still shocked. Lodges covered the plain. This was one of the largest, perhaps *the* largest, gathering of Indians in western history.

This is the village that you're going to attack, Mr. Custer? If I could only hit you with a board up the side of your head and get your attention and tell you what's coming, I would welcome the opportunity. Meaningless, of course.

He pondered. The strange thing about what was about to happen is that until just recently, most Sioux and Cheyenne in the region had no hostile intentions. There had been sporadic violent encounters between the army and tribes, for sure, but the tribes were accustomed to sporadic violence. It wasn't unusual. Now, in late spring of 1876, most were busy hunting or otherwise going about their lives. They had no thoughts of war. It was only the whites, the army officers, and the politicians who wanted war.

Winnie touched his arm. He looked abruptly at her, roused from his reflection. They stood before a large lodge. The warrior they had followed held the flap at the opening. Brett bent and went inside. Winnie followed.

Inside, they saw about fifteen men sitting silently in a circle around a low fire. All looked up at the newcomers. Their faces were blank, betraying no hostility, rather curiosity. The guide showed Brett and Winona their places at the fire circle. When they were seated, the guide spoke softly to Winona.

She bent toward Brett. "He say it okay with other people when I tell you what they say." He nodded to her and to the faces that silently watched them.

Then a man who sat across the fire from Brett spoke, looking alternately into the fire, up to the lodge peak, and to the others in the circle.

Brett gaped. *Sitting Bull!* He looked exactly as he did in the many pictures he had seen of the Sioux chieftain. The mouth turned down at the corners in a seeming frown, strong facial features, a single feather in his straight hair. Though Brett had hoped, even expected, to see him in this encampment, he was still stunned to be sitting in his presence. He had long been convinced that Sitting Bull was one of the most interesting figures in western American history, a true American patriot. He grimaced when he remembered what lay ahead for him.

Sitting Bull spoke to Winona, looking from her to Brett. The chief finished speaking and looked into the fire. Winnie leaned toward Brett and spoke softly. "Sitting Bull say he speak to you now. I think he know some English, but he say he not like English. If he speak in Sioux, he say I can tell you what he say."

While Winona spoke to Brett, Sitting Bull turned to the man beside him, and they talked softly.

Brett frowned. *I have seen pictures of that man beside Sitting Bull.* He searched his memory. *Is it... yes! It is Crazy Horse! Of course, he was one of the principal leaders in the fight against Custer.*

Then Sitting Bull took the pipe that lay in front of him. Picking up a burning stick from the fire, he lit the pipe. He puffed until the tobacco glowed. He offered the pipe to the four winds, the Earth and the sky, then offered it to Brett. Taking the pipe, Brett puffed a few times and returned it to Sitting Bull. The chief then offered it to Crazy Horse, who drew on it and passed it to the man beside him. The pipe was handed off until it had passed to each person in the circle. When it returned to Sitting Bull, he knocked out the ashes and laid it on the ground before him.

Brett suddenly realized that Sitting Bull was looking directly at him and speaking in Sioux.

Winona touched Brett's arm and leaned to him,

speaking softly. "He say I said you have big medicine and know what is going to happen. He is glad to hear this and wants you to tell him things. He say his people will fight soldiers in big battle. He ask who is going to win."

Brett inhaled deeply. "Tell him—"

"Stop!" Sitting Bull said in English, then reverted to Sioux. He spoke at length to Winona, finished, and looked again into the fire.

"He say your medicine let you see what is going to happen. But does your medicine let you change what is going to happen?"

"Hmm. You know the answer to that. Tell him I cannot change what is going to happen."

Winona translated Brett's words. Sitting Bull nodded grimly and spoke to her. She turned to Brett. "He say if you cannot change what is going to happen, he not want to know what you see."

Sitting Bull spoke again, this time speaking into the fire, not looking at Winona or Brett. He spoke with passion, rocking back and forth, looking only into the fire. Others sitting around the fire circle listened intently, sometimes glancing at each other, then staring at Sitting Bull. Then he was finished. He glanced at Winona, then looked back into the flames.

Winona translated. "Sitting Bull say he also have big medicine. He say when he was coming to this camp, he had vision." She described the vision slowly, trying to remember Sitting Bull's words. Sitting on a rock in the wilderness, praying to Wakan Tanka, the Great Spirit, Sitting Bull slept and dreamed. In the dream, a dense cloud of dust was pushed by strong winds from the east. From the opposite direction, fierce winds propelled a pure white cloud. The two clouds collided, producing explosive thunder, shooting lightning and sheets of rain. Then the storm ended, the dust cloud dissipated, and the white cloud drifted toward the east.

Winona continued. Later, in camp, Sitting Bull said, he explained the vision to the chiefs. The dust cloud was the soldiers, the white cloud the Sioux and Cheyenne. The vision told him that the soldiers were coming from the east to wipe out the village, but they would fail. The Sioux considered Sitting Bull a holy man in perfect harmony with Wakan Tanka, and they believed the lesson of the vision.

When Winona had finished translating to Brett, she looked at Sitting Bull. The chief spoke again, and she translated. Just days ago, Sitting Bull had taken part in a sun dance in which he was ritually pierced a hundred times in his arms and tiny bits of flesh cut away. In the ensuing delirium, he saw soldiers and their animals, upside down, falling into the village. This vision, Sitting Bull said, predicted defeat of the soldiers and victory for the tribes.

Brett listened intently, head lowered, eyes closed. He had always been fascinated with the visions of Sitting Bull and used them in his lectures as powerful evidence of the beliefs and leadership of the chief.

Sitting Bull said Winona's name and continued speaking, pointing repeatedly at Brett. She looked at Brett, nodded, then back to Sitting Bull. She said something briefly to Sitting Bull, nodded again.

Sitting Bull stood, others followed, and the gathering broke up. Winona walked to the lodge opening, and Brett went after her.

As they walked toward their lodge, Brett asked

Winona about her last exchange with Sitting Bull. "It seemed to be something about me. He kept pointing at me."

"Yes. He say if you walk around village without me, somebody shoot you. He say he will give you something to wear so people know you are friend."

———

That evening, sitting at a small fire at their lodge, they watched a young warrior coming. He carried something with both hands Stopping before them, he handed the package to Winona, said something in Sioux, and pointed at Brett. She took the package and replied in Sioux. He turned and walked away.

Winona unrolled a breastplate and smiled. "Look. This very good." The breastplate featured two rows of long bones of buffalo and birds, separated by a short row of bones in the middle. Buckskin tassels lined the sides. "Look," she said again, "this string goes around your neck, and these," showing him, "go around your waist." She held up the breastplate to his chest, tied the band around his neck, crawled around to his back, and tied the waistband. She came back to his front and admired the plate. "Now every person will know you are friend and welcome in the village."

Brett ran his hand lightly over the breastplate. "I feel safer already." He pulled Winona to him and kissed her.

They sat in silence, staring into the fire. Brett's mind had been racing all day as he tried to calculate when Custer would attack. Winona had translated conversations she heard on several occasions since their arrival in camp. He learned that Sitting Bull and Crazy Horse had taken part just days ago in a fierce battle. He wondered whether this could have been the fight against General Crook on the Rosebud. While both sides suffered casualties, it could only be called an Indian victory, sufficient to give Crook pause.

Brett remembered from the histories that the general decided that he would not take the offensive until he received reinforcements. Thus, he would not commit his force in the final battles of the campaign which culminated at the Little Bighorn. If this indeed were the fight with Crook, this meant Custer's attack would come very soon.

Meanwhile, the village and its population continued to increase. Warriors from the agencies rode into the village. Their coming coincided with the arrival of bands of hunters who had received news of an impending major confrontation with the army. In just a few days, the village had doubled in size to a thousand lodges, as many as 7,000 people and 1,800 warriors.

Brett shook his head. *If Custer had not been in such a hurry, his task might have been easier. The accumulation of great numbers of people and animals in the massive village had cleaned the vicinity of game. Grasslands had been grazed off for miles around. Leaders soon would have been forced to scatter to other sites to find game and grass. This knowledge might have convinced a rational army commander to wait for a more propitious moment to attack. Custer was not rational.*

He could not help comparing the leadership of the two commanders of the approaching conflict. Like most military commanders, Custer led by absolute authority and the threat of punishment for failure to follow orders. Sitting Bull, like most Indian chiefs, led by influence and persuasion.

Sitting Bull's leadership style indeed was demonstrated in the recent action against General Crook's force. Sitting Bull, supported by Crazy Horse, wished to avoid a confrontation. He told his warriors to leave the soldiers alone unless they attacked the village. Excited young men, anxious to prove themselves, ignored the chiefs and prepared for battle. A band of five hundred rode from the village in darkness. Sitting Bull and Crazy Horse, undoubtedly caught up in the excitement, joined the young men and took part in the battle that followed.

Would Custer react in the same way if he had ordered his men to hold the line, and a bunch of excitable young recruits decided that it would be great fun to attack an Indian village? He would probably have them shot.

He looked up to see Winona staring at him across the campfire. "Come over here, sweetheart." She stood, came over and sat beside him. She picked up a stick and stirred the coals, picked up a handful of sticks and dropped them on the low flames.

He leaned over and kissed her cheek, looked back at the fire where flames flickered from the nest of dry sticks. "There will be no winner here," he said.

She frowned, looked up at him. "I don't understand. You said the tribes will win."

He put an arm around her shoulders, pulled her to him, stared into the fire. He spoke slowly, softly, sadly. "The tribes will win the battle, but the army, the government, the politicians, they will be infuriated. They will decide that Indian resistance to the white American occupation of the western lands must be finished, once and for all. They will say that the tribes that occupy these lands must be finally defeated, either by persuasion or by war, and made to live on reservations. They will no longer be free to move about, no longer permitted to follow the buffalo and the seasons. They will be forced to become farmers, or they will become paupers, fed by the government."

They were silent, staring at the flames. "You have seen this?" she said.

"Yes. I have seen it. This is what happens."

"What can we do?"

He was still, quiet. She looked up at him, holding his arm with both hands. He spoke slowly, frowning. "The books tell about the course of this battle and something of the two sides in the battle, but they do not, they *cannot*, tell *everything*. The books do not mention Brett Davis and Winona, but we are here. What can we do that is not mentioned in the books?"

They alternately stared into the flames and up to the clear dark sky, stars pulsing brightly. She turned to him. "How 'bout children? And their mothers? Do the books tell what happens to women and children? Many women and children were killed at Sand Creek. Can we do something here?"

He looked down at her, frowning, paused. "I have never seen any account that tells in any detail what happens to the women and children. The books say that the women take down lodges when their men go off to fight, but the accounts say little about them after that. Maybe we can do something to encourage or even arrange their movement from the camp before the battles begin. What do you think? Would they listen to us?"

"There is no plan, I think. The women just know that they must take down lodges when they know their village is going to be attacked, or when their men go off to fight."

Brett stared into the darkness. *But when will Custer attack? Following good army protocol, in the past he always attacked at first light, hoping to surprise the enemy. That won't happen this time. He will become impatient. When scouts see parties of Indians ahead, Custer will realize the army has been seen, and he will decide to attack at once. He will not wait until the next day at dawn. He will attack just past midday, expecting to destroy the village and its defenders before sunset.*

He will attack on June 25. Is that tomorrow? He instinctively thrust a hand into his pants pocket for the cell phone that was always there. "Dammit!"

"What's wrong?" Winona said.

"I'm trying to decide when the army will attack the village. I think it is tomorrow."

———

Dawn. Brett worked on building a fire. Winona usually had a fire going before he awakened, but this morning was different. He hardly slept. He could not know the date, but his calculation, working backward to Abilene where he had seen a calendar, suggested that this was the day Custer would attack.

The day began like any other, women cooking, mending, working on stretched hides beside lodges. Children splashed in the shallows of the river nearby.

Many men, exhausted from dancing through the night, slept in their lodges. Others, particularly young warriors, had ponies tethered near their lodges, prepared and eager to defend the village. However, since there was no anticipation of early contact with an enemy, most of the horses were on sparse grass outside the village.

Brett stood beside his fire, looking down the lane between rows of lodges, uneasy in spite of the calm that pervaded the village. At a sound from his lodge, he turned to see Winona stepping through the opening, running fingers through her long hair with both hands. She smiled, came to him and kissed him. She bent to pick up a handful of dry sticks.

Both looked sharply at a young man who ran from the riverbank into the heart of the village, shouting. Then two women ran from the river, shouting. People stopped their cooking and mending, others came out of lodges, all ran toward those who sounded the alarm.

"What are they saying?" said Brett.

"The soldiers are coming! They are shooting!" she said.

Men rushed from lodges carrying weapons, running for their ponies on the riverbank. They frantically painted themselves and their horses for battle. Mounting quickly, they held bows and rifles high and kicked their horses into a gallop toward the river.

Women called children to come from the shallows and banks to prepare for flight. Some women and old men stood rooted in the midst of the confusion, singing death songs for their warriors. Others, following habit, hurriedly began taking down lodges and building travois for the move.

Winona and Brett ran through the village, urging women to find their children and flee. Winona shouted that their children were more important than their lodges. You can build another lodge, she said; you cannot replace a child. Go! Run!

Some women ignored her entreaties; others dropped poles and hides and fled, calling their children to follow. Some warriors pulled family members onto their horses and galloped to hills where they left them and returned to the village. Brett recalled that Sitting Bull carried his wife and sister to safety before riding to the battle site.

Brett and Winona watched the village emptying, some women and children running to the hills, warriors toward the battle lines. "Let's do what we can here," Brett said. They rode toward the fleeing mothers with children. "Tell them we want to help." She yelled to them, and they slowed. Brett reined up and lifted a child to straddle in front of him on the saddle, then pulled up the mother behind him. Winona did the same, pulling up a child and showing the mother how to put her foot into the stirrup. They rode at a slow lope toward the hills where they had seen others running.

They dropped over a rising to a hollow where about two dozen women, children and old men sat and stood, apprehensive, watching them come. Winona called to them to assure them they were friends, invited to the village by Sitting Bull. They dismounted, and Winnie showed them the breastplate that Brett wore.

Suddenly half a dozen soldiers burst over the crest of the rising and looked down on the people in the hollow. They reined up, some pulling pistols, others drawing sabers. Seeing only women and children and decrepit old men, they hesitated.

"Do we do it, Jimmy?" shouted a soldier.

Brett recognized Jimmy, the corporal who brought them meals. "Don't do this, Jimmy!" Brett shouted. "They're children and women! Don't do it!"

"No, Jimmy!" shouted Winona.

The soldiers' skittish horses danced about in the shouting. Soldiers waited for the corporal's order. "Do it, dammit! Do it!" said a soldier, his face contorted. He fired his pistol, and a woman fell.

Instantly, the soldier was blown backward from Brett's shot. He dropped the pistol and grabbed his shoulder, struggling to control his skittish horse.

"Stop firing!" said Jimmy. "Pull back! Stop firing!" He looked directly at Winona, then jerked his mount's reins and whirled around. "Pull back!" The other soldiers reined after him, and they disappeared behind the rising.

Silence but for the faint hoofbeats of the soldiers' horses. All in the swale stood rigid, staring at the rising where the soldiers had disappeared. Winona ran to the woman who had been shot. She lay on the ground, unconscious, blood seeping from her side. Two women nearby knelt and began to treat the wound. One said something to Winona in Sioux.

"She say it not bad, just cut," Winona said to Brett. Brett nodded, took Winona's arm, and they went to their horses. He untied the reins from the sapling. She took her reins, hesitated. "I remember stories you tell about this fight. I hope Jimmy not die." He hesitated a moment, then mounted. She followed, and they galloped toward the village.

———

Staying close to their lodge, Brett and Winona watched warriors returning to the village, shouting their successes, telling what happened to them, what they saw, whooping about valor and coups and soldiers falling to their arrows and bullets. The battle continued for the remainder of the day and resumed at sunrise.

At mid-morning, an excited band of a dozen warriors galloped into the village, whipping their horses, shouting.

"They say Long Hair dead," said Winona. "Who is Long Hair?" She turned see Brett staring into the distance, in the direction of the battlefield.

"Honey?" she said.

"Long Hair. That's what they call Custer. Custer is dead. It's finished. He was killed on the field with all of the members of his command. When the stories of this campaign are written, this will be called The Battle of the Little Bighorn."

Winona and Brett stood at their lodge, still watching the warriors shouting and crying their successes. "They very happy," she said.

Brett, grim, glanced aside at her, then to a trio of young men, whipping their mounts up the lane, yelling and whooping. The three men pulled up before them. One spoke excitedly to Winnie, barely controlling his skittish horse. Brett recognized the young warrior who had first taken them to meet Sitting Bull. A moment later, he whooped and the three kicked their horses to a gallop down the lane.

She watched them, then turned to Brett. "He say he so happy at winning fight with soldiers. He say soldiers in other battles killed some of his family and most of his friends. He say we should go to place where they fought today."

Brett frowned. Winona waited, but he said nothing. "Honey, I want to see," she said.

"You want to see dead soldiers?"

"Honey, I see so many times after battles with soldiers, many of my people, my family and my friends, dead, killed by soldiers. It not dead soldiers I want to see now. I want to see end of a fight my people win. I want to see." She walked toward her horse, still saddled and reins tied where they had left the mounts in case they had to leave quickly.

He hesitated only a beat, then strode to the horses and untied reins. They mounted and rode in the opposite direction of dozens of returning warriors, still excited and shouting their valor and victory. Brett figured these were among the last to leave the field, busy with scalping and taking anything of value from the corpses.

Winona and Brett rode from a pine copse and reined up. She gasped at the scene on the gently sloping meadow opposite. On the field of dry summer grasses and stunted sagebrush, scattered corpses lay in disarray, some in blue uniform, most partly stripped to pink skin, already beginning to burn in the hot sun. A few Indians, women and old men, wandered among the dead, occasionally bending to pluck something from a body.

Winona rocked in her saddle. "I see dead people after fights before, but not so many. Not so many."

Brett stared at the field. "One hundred ninety-seven soldiers were killed here today. So the record says. The army will not forget." He turned to her. "Winnie, we must think about leaving soon. Another army force is coming. They will see this field and the bodies."

———

Brett and Winona sat at their fire circle, staring into the flames that sizzled with the juices dripping from the rabbit roasting on the wooden spit. They looked up occasionally, listening to the singing, shouts, revelry of the victorious warriors at many fire circles.

"It will be a short celebration," he said. "Scouts will tell them of the approach of more soldiers. They will not worry so much since they still have any army force outnumbered. But when the excitement of the Custer battle passes, they will turn back to the life of the village. They will realize that food is short, for themselves and their horses, and they will move the village to hunt for buffalo.

"Winnie, the army and government in Washington will be so outraged by Custer's defeat that they will send larger armies into Indian country. In the months ahead, there will be battles, and the overwhelming numbers and power of the army will defeat the warriors.

"For a time, it will appear that many Sioux, following Sitting Bull, will find a new life by going to Canada. They will find plenty of buffalo and a warm welcome from Canadian officials. But relations go bad as buffalo numbers decline, and Canadian Indians complain about the competition from American tribes. Then American officials will demand the Sioux return and surrender. Sitting Bull and other leaders will refuse, but they eventually have no choice. They will return and be assigned to reservations. It is a very sad time for the plains tribes."

Brett remembered how Sitting Bull would progress from this point, from the leading spiritual and war leader of the Sioux people to a circus buffoon, lionized by a curious public, but a buffoon nevertheless. His bizarre participation in Buffalo Bill's Wild West show in the East for a season was humiliating. Brett decided he would say nothing to Winnie about this. Maybe later, but not now.

————

The condition and prospects of the tribes changed quickly after the defeat of Custer. Hunters returned to the village with little meat and hides. Rumors of large army forces approaching were unnerving. Some warriors, passing Brett in the village, looked hard at him, their faces clouded. He still wore Sitting Bull's breastplate, but he was white, and with the threat posed by the army, the previous acceptance of this white man in their midst appeared shaky.

Brett and Winona sat on the riverbank on a sunny afternoon. A dozen horses drank from the stream on the opposite bank. Brett watched the horses, then stared at the herd that grazed beyond the stream.

"You worry," Winona said.

He turned to her. He nodded, looked back to the stream. "Yes, I worry. I think I am no longer welcome here. And I worry about what will happen when the next army arrives."

Why am I cursed by knowing what will happen?

"I think we should go," he said. "At least, I should

go. If you want to stay, you should. It would break my heart, but you should do what you think is best for you." He looked at the stream, shook his head. "I have no idea what is going to happen to me. I think about it every day. I could disappear any minute or dry up and blow away like dead leaves. I don't know what I am, Winnie, why I'm here, and what will happen to me. I'm not... real, Winnie. I'm a phantom. I could disappear any minute. Maybe you should stay with your people, and I will go."

"Stop that! I don't like hear that talk." She took his arm, leaned against his shoulder. "I could not go away. Where you go, I go. Honey sweetheart." She ducked her head, smiled.

He took her in his arms and held her, his face in her hair. Leaning back, he put his hands to her cheeks, kissed her lips. "Then we will go together. Honey sweetheart. If you decided to stay, I would will myself to... I don't know what... evaporate, become a shadow, or a wisp of vapor and vanish in the wind."

She kissed him. "I don't understand."

"I don't want you to understand." He stood and took her hand, pulling her up. "We will leave tomorrow morning, after others are up. If we left in the dark, we could be shot as an enemy. I want people to see us leaving."

———

They rode in a flat between ranges of low hills. He led a packhorse he bought the previous day from a young warrior. He paid with a thin gold ring he had worn on his little finger. His mother gave it to him as a child, explaining that it came from some relative that even she could not remember. He hated to give it up now, but he owned nothing else of value but his clothes and his weapons, and he could not let them go. The warrior seemed pleased with the transaction.

"Where are we going?" Winona said.

"I don't know. Some safe place, I hope. Right now, I'm looking for a rabbit I can shoot for supper." He looked at her.

She screwed up her face. He smiled.

———

They sat on the ground at a small fire that cast its light only a few feet in the gloaming. The remains of a roasted prairie chicken lay on a flat rock at the edge of the fire. Each held a chunk of chicken, tearing hot slivers from bones. Winona finished the piece she held and rubbed her hands on grass at her side.

"Better than rabbit," she said.

"Yes, I know." He dropped a backbone on the fire and wiped his hands on the grass. Standing with a grunt, he checked the three horses that were hobbled nearby while Winona stood and walked into the darkness.

He looked at the western horizon where a thin layer of yellow light lay between the dark sky and the gray plain. A hint of a breeze, a cool vapor, touched his cheeks. *How can such perfection exist in a world that is full of so much evil?* After a long moment, he went to the pack and pulled out blankets, spread them on the ground beside the fire.

She walked into the circle of firelight. "Where we go tomorrow?"

"Don't know. We're in a large place called Montana Territory right now. I don't suppose that means anything to you. We could head south, looking for somewhere that won't be as cold as this country is gonna be in a few months. Or we could head for some town, if I can remember where there are towns in Montana in 1876. A town would be safer than the countryside in the battles that are coming between the army and the tribes." He paused, waiting for a reply. She simply looked at him. "What do you think?" he said.

"I go where you go."

He took her in his arms and held her, looking over her shoulder into the darkness.

CHAPTER 8

B rett awoke to absolute silence. Unusual. Most mornings, he was awakened by birdsong. He sat up, stretched and yawned. He threw off the covers and stood. Shivering, he bent and picked up his coat, struggled into it. His eyes suddenly opened wide. He saw riders, about a dozen, less than a hundred yards away, moving slowly across the meadow. *Surely they have seen our horses, if not us. But they're not coming this way. They're passing us.*

Hold on! He saw more riders, a half a dozen or so, behind the first bunch, moving in the same direction. He turned around, preparing to wake Winona, and came up short. On the other side of their camp, he saw three small groups of riders moving in the same direction as the others. Beyond them, he saw what appeared to be more bunches, most riding but some walking, all moving west.

He sat on the bed, pulled on his pants, then his boots, stood and buttoned his pants. Striding to his saddlebag on the ground near the hobbled horses, he pulled out the binocular and looked at the moving groups on each side of their camp. None of the riders or walkers looked his way, though he was sure that some among them must have seen the two strangers and their horses.

Wait a minute. In his surprise at seeing the riders and trying to guess their meaning, he had overlooked the land. *It's different. We rode yesterday in a grassy prairie between two low ridges, high mountains in the distance. All I see now is a sandy flat of sparse short grass, scattered sage, cactus and other plants native to desert. No trees or mountains in sight.*

He slumped. *Again. Where this time? God in heaven, where this time?* He whirled around. *Winnie!* He saw her, still there, under the blanket. He knelt and touched her face, leaned down and kissed her cheek.

She stirred, opened her eyes, blinking. She took his hand, a hint of a smile. "That nice way to wake up." She kissed his hand. Pushing the covers down, she pulled on her boots and stood.

"Winnie, there's something strange going on."

She put up a hand to refuse the proffered binocular. "Wait a minute." She ran behind a nearby bush. A moment later, she walked back to him, smoothing her dress.

"Cold," she said. He held out her coat, and she pulled it on. She frowned at him. "What?" He offered the binocular again and pointed.

She looked through the binocular at the lines of people on both sides of the camp, moving westward, eyes ahead, none looking their way.

"What do you make of it?" he said.

She lowered the binocular, frowned, still looking at

the passing throng. "I not sure." She pondered. "Maybe they go to a meeting of tribes." She paused. "Or important dance."

Brett listened, but his mind wandered. He closed his eyes and rubbed his forehead. *Again.* He shook his head slowly. Opening his eyes, he saw Winona watching him, silent, understanding.

He put his arms around her shoulders. "You know, don't you." She nodded. "It's happened again. I'm beyond wondering and worrying since there is nothing I can do about it. All I know at this moment is that we are transported somewhere, and you are with me. At this point, I think I would shoot myself if you weren't with me."

"Don't *say* that. If I wake up and you gone, I find bad spirit and kill him."

He smiled. "My, my, I think you would. I feel sorry for the bad spirit already."

She ducked her head, buried her face in the folds of his shirt against his chest. She gripped handfuls of his shirt and pulled him to her. "Why this happen to us? Why us?"

He put his arms around her shoulders, closed his eyes and held her. He took her face in his hands, kissed her lips lightly. "I can't answer that. It's all my fault, my curiosity. But sweetheart, I can bear anything as long as I can touch you. I'm sorry I have caused you so much pain."

"You talk silly. You just be sure take me with you when cos-thing take you some place."

He smiled. "Well, cos-thing has transported us to this place." He looked around at the mass of people moving in the same direction. "The only way for us to find out where we are is to join the exodus. Okay?"

"Yes. We go with them." She looked up at him. "What is 'exodus'?"

"Sorry. A bunch of people going in the same direction. Going away from something or to something. I suspect these people are going to something. And we're going with them. They have taken no notice of us, and I think they will not be bothered by our moving in the same direction."

———

For the rest of the day, Brett and Winona walked, leading the horses, at the same pace and in the same direction as the groups on each side of them. More groups appeared from each side and joined the march. The lines of riders and walkers now appeared as spokes in a wagon wheel, moving toward a distant center. None in the groups seemed to pay any attention to the two strangers. Nobody approached them, nor did they shy away from them.

At dusk, the Indian groups stopped, built campfires, and settled down for the night. Brett and Winona did as well. Brett thought that now someone from the groups would come to inquire about the two strangers, but no one came.

Next morning, all of the groups broke camp in good order and were soon moving. At high noon, Brett and Winona walked over a low rising and saw in the distance a large concentration of people, hundreds if not thousands, clustered around a small open space. The spokes converged at the mass, the hub.

"I may be the only white man here. Should I wear the breastplate?" Brett said.

She frowned, pondered. "No. Somebody may think you killed Indian man and took it off his body. Just stay close to me."

He smiled. "I can do that."

Mounting, they rode down the slope of the rising, mixing with others riding and walking in the same direction. The others glanced briefly at the white man and Indian woman traveling side-by-side but wasted no time on them.

They rode toward a distant large gathering of people crowded around the small open space in the center of the hub. Brett and Winona dismounted, and he tied the reins to a dry sage bush. Dozens of horses were tied to bushes nearby. Their owners walked, silently for the most part, toward the center of the mass, the open space. Brett and Winona followed.

"Ask them what this is about," said Brett. "What will we see ahead?"

She spoke in Arapaho to a man walking alongside. He shook his head. She switched to Sioux. Another shake of the head. She walked over to a woman and asked the same question, in Arapaho, Cheyenne, and Sioux with the same result.

She went back to Brett, shaking her head. A man who walked behind the woman and overheard their conversation walked over to Winnie. "You speak English? Or him?" pointing at Brett.

"Yes!" Winona said and stepped aside, deferring to Brett.

"I speak English," Brett said. "What goes on here? What is in the circle ahead?"

"Wovoka," the man said. "Do you know Wovoka?"

Brett recoiled, stopped dead in his tracks, his jaw hanging. *Wovoka.* He looked up at the heavens, closed his eyes.

Winona stopped beside him, watching. She took his arm. "Are you okay?"

He nodded.

"Do you know Wovoka?" the man said again.

"Yes... I know about Wovoka," Brett said. Winona turned to him, her face blank.

The man waited, but when Brett said no more, he walked ahead.

"Who is Wovoka?" Winona said.

They walked, but more slowly.

"You know how I know about Wovoka?" he said. She nodded. He stopped. "We don't need to see Wovoka today. There're too many people up there. We'll see him another day, perhaps tomorrow." He took her arm, and they turned back.

————

Winona and Brett sat at their small fire circle. The glow of many campfires softly illuminated the landscape in all directions.

"Where are we?" she said.

Brett inhaled deeply, exhaled. "We are in the state of Nevada. That is south and west of Montana where we were before. The year is 1890, near the end of the period whites call the Old West. Whites will look back and think of the Old West with mixed feelings, some sad memories, but mostly happy memories.

"Indian people also will have mixed feeling about

this time. They will remember happy times before whites invaded their lands, but times got worse and worse, and in 1890, conditions were so bad, Indian people were desperate." He stared into the fire.

"Tell me about Wovoka."

"Wovoka. He is a holy man of sorts. He is Paiute, never away from the valley where he was born and raised. His father died when he was just a boy, and a white couple took him in and raised him. He was exposed to the white man's ways, including their religion. These white people were Christians, Presbyterians, and he learned from them to read the Bible every day. But he did not forget his Indian upbringing.

"As Wovoka told it, when he was a young man, he began to have visions. He says he was lifted to heaven where he saw God. He also saw all the Indian people who had died long ago and now in heaven were happy and enjoying the old ways. God told Wovoka to go back to Earth, tell Indian people to put war aside, love everybody, including white people, and live in peace forever.

"More to the point, God told Wovoka that Earth was to be reborn and given back to the Indians. The dead ancestors were going to return to Earth in youth and strength. The buffalo were going to come back in their great herds. This is what Wovoka said.

"To bring all this to pass, Wovoka said, the people must perform a ceremonial dance which he described. He told them they must perform the dance five nights in a row. The more often they did the dance, the sooner the rebirth he described would come.

"He said all this at first to the Paiutes, his own people. It wasn't long before Paiute men, believers, went out to other tribes and told them about Wovoka's visions. I suppose people of my day would call these messengers 'missionaries'. This promise of rebirth swept the West."

She frowned. "Why? What do you mean, it swept the West?"

He paused, frowning. "Throughout history, everywhere in the world, people who have suffered for many years and see no hope eventually look for help from a higher power. In their despair, Indian people everywhere began to believe Wovoka and his visions. They began to perform the dance that he described."

Brett closed his eyes, looked up. He had always been profoundly moved by the stories of Wovoka and his visions. He marveled that he remembered so much.

He leaned toward Winona. "I was impressed, saddened actually, when I read about a chant some Arapahos sang when they danced. I was so impressed I never forgot it:

> *My Father, have pity on me,*
> *I have nothing to eat,*
> *I am dying of thirst,*
> *Everything is gone.*

"Whites called Wovoka's ritual the Ghost Dance since it predicted the return of dead people." He shook his head, sighed heavily.

Winona held his hand, pressed it to her cheek.

He stared into the fire, shaking his head slowly. "Sometimes I get so sad and angry at the same time when I think about what happened to Indian people in general in this country, but especially in the West. There have been times during lectures that I get so angry I have to stop, breathe deeply and apologize to my students."

He paused, rocking forward and backward. "You know how the army and government have treated Indian people badly. There is more. The army and government were just agents of change. You know how much your people depended on the buffalo. White settlement and the railroad had begun to reduce the numbers of buffalo by the time of the battle at the Bighorn. In the years following, whites hunted buffalo for hides, and the buffalo are almost wiped out. Remember, I said the year now, today, is 1890. The buffalo are almost gone. I doubt we will see buffalo again."

Her mouth opened wide. "I... don't understand. How can buffalo go away? There are so many. They are like stars in the sky, like raindrops in a storm." She turned to him for a response, but he simply stared at the embers.

"There's still something else I haven't mentioned, the invention of barbed wire. That's a wire made of metal with sharp metal pins on it. The farm where you lived with the white people had a corral made of wooden poles to hold horses, didn't it?"

"Yes."

"A barbed wire fence is like a big corral, stretching long distances, to hold cattle. Barbed wire fences prevented buffalo moving freely, and they prevent Indian people from moving along trails they had followed forever.

"It's all so bad, Winnie. The army, white settlers, barbed wire, hide hunters. Indian people were forced onto reservations where government said they would be housed and fed and given pieces of land and taught to be farmers. None of this happened. The promise to teach them farming was almost never kept. Rations are cut repeatedly until they will be reduced to half.

"The condition of plains Indians gradually worsened. Last year and this year, there have been deadly outbreaks of terrible diseases—measles, influenza and whooping cough—that have killed many people, mostly on reservations. These deaths are blamed on whites who they caught the diseases from.

"Can you see why Indian people are so eager to follow Wovoka? The people had given up hope, and he promises a new hope. He promises a return to the old ways."

The depths of their despair are so deep that they would believe the visions of a deluded or deranged man who knew precious little of the intimate Indian way since he had lived in a white man's house most of his life.

Brett slumped, drained. He embraced her and rested his head on her shoulder.

She held his arm with both hands. "Can we go see Wovoka tomorrow?"

How can I allow her to hope when I know where Wovoka and the Ghost Dance are going?

"Yes, we will see him tomorrow."

———

Next morning, Winona and Brett stood near the front of the throng that had begun gathering at sunrise. The dance was already underway when they arrived. They were immediately mesmerized by the spectacle and watched in silence as dancers, side-by side and holding hands, moved in a slow circle, shuffling, sliding. All wore eagle feathers in their hair, including the women.

"I never see women wear feathers before in dance," said Winona.

"All dancers have to wear feathers," he said. "It is the feathers that will lift the dancers, the faithful, to a safe place when soil rolls down over the country to bury the unbelievers and all white people. Do you see why whites will call this a war dance?"

She looked at him, frowning. "A war dance? Why?"

"Because it predicts that dead Indians will come back to life, and whites will disappear. The whites will figure that could never happen without an all-out war on whites."

"No, no, it cannot be a war dance. Look." She pointed toward the dancers. "Women are dancing. Women do not dance in war dances."

Brett frowned, listening. "Winnie, what are they singing now, the same words, over and over?"

She listened, leaning forward, frowning. After a couple of minutes, she translated. "They sing:

> *Father, I come*
> *Mother, I come*
> *Brother, I come*
> *Father give us back our arrows."*

"There's the problem, Winnie. Wovoka says to love white people and get along with them while teaching that whites will just...disappear. But the chant just now asks for their arrows to be returned. Whites will see that as longing for the means to fight."

"But...but, they follow Wovoka, and he does not call for war on whites."

"Okay," said Brett. "I understand, but this is all new. Wovoka's message is different from anything Indian people have heard before. The old ceremonial rules don't apply. No religious leader has ever predicted the departed will rise from the dead and whites will disappear.

"Wovoka said men and women should dance together, and that's what is happening. Anyway, whites who hear the message of Wovoka are terrified, and they'll believe what they want to believe."

She frowned. "I understand." She took his arm, and they moved through the spectators to the front of the throng. She leaned forward, her face tense as she watched and listened.

The dancers, men and women, many dressed in white and holding hands, bobbed and twisted. They leaned forward, eyes closed, shuffling sideways, hardly lifting their feet off the ground. The men were mostly silent while women made a shrill yelping call. Then they chanted in unison. Winona strained to hear the words of the chant, constant and repetitive. She pulled Brett to her and spoke softly. "They sing in Sioux language. They say:

> I see my father,
> I see my mother,
> I see my brother,
> I see my sister."

———

That evening, Brett and Winona sat at their campfire, eating the last of the prairie chicken they had roasted for dinner last evening. During their walk from the dance ground to their camp, Winona had talked excitedly about the spectacle of the dance and the watchers.

Now, she was quiet, tearing off slivers of chicken, raising her head to listen to conversation from nearby camps, staring into the flickering fire.

Brett waited. His mind raced as he speculated on what observations she might make, what questions she might ask, and how he would respond.

Finally, she dropped the clean chicken bones on the embers and wiped her hands on the dry grass.

Here it comes.

"I remember what Sitting Bull say to you. He say if you can't change what is going to happen, he not want you to say anything about what is going to happen. You say Wovoka's vision and the dance he tells about is going to spread all over the country. I not going to ask you what is going to happen. Don't say what is going to happen. I don't want to know."

Whew.

"Wovoka has very strong medicine," she said. "I understand why people who have suffered so much want to believe him."

He watched her as she prepared for bed. She kissed him and went to her blankets. He saw in the dancing firelight that she lay on her back, eyes open.

———

They arrived at the dance site early and stood at the front of the crowd of watchers. Dancers were just beginning to form into the circle, some moving rhythmically, turning, bending, twisting, murmuring to others around them.

Winona took Brett's arm, looked up at him. "Honey sweetheart, I going to dance. I hope that okay with you?"

He stiffened, then relaxed immediately. "Of course, it's okay. I will watch from here."

"You okay by yourself? A white man by hisself?"

He smiled, pondered, looking up and frowning. "I am... um... a newspaperman from the *Chicago Tribune*. I'm here to tell the world about Wovoka and his message. If anyone questions me, I will point to you in the circle, my interpreter. You go on. I'll be okay."

Squeezing his arm, she stepped slowly away. She looked back at him, approaching the circle of players that had begun the dance, swaying, shuffling, twisting, women wailing. She waited a moment, then stepped into the line, moving slowly at first, watching, imitating those around her, then more confidently, bending, twisting, shuffling, moving now as if she had been dancing for days.

He lowered his head, frowning. *Oh, my, my, my. My Cheyenne sweetheart wants so much to believe. What have I done?*

The dance continued as the sun rose, more people stepping into the circle, moving as if there was no end, shuffling, whirling, arms waving, women wailing, an occasional sharp shout.

Then it ended abruptly. The dancers stopped, stood in place, drooping, breathing deeply. They recovered, dispersed, and walked to family or friends waiting in the crowd of onlookers.

Winona hurried to Brett. Smiling broadly, she took his hand. "Honey sweetheart, I meet man from village at Bighorn. He say he glad to see me. I tell him you here, too. He say he and friends go to his village at Standing Rock reservation. He ask us go with him. He say others from Bighorn village are there." Her eyes opened wide. "He say Sitting Bull there!"

———

Winona roused Brett at first light next day. She had learned Wovoka would talk at sunup with any who wished to take part in an informal discussion. By the time they arrived, Winona pulling the sleepy Brett by the sleeve, a large following had gathered. Wovoka stood in the center of the open space, speaking confidently, responding to questions. Winona pulled Brett along, edging their way up near the front.

Winona leaned forward, intent on catching questions and comments from bystanders and Wovoka's responses. After a series of questions and responses, Winona whispered into Brett's ear.

It seems that Wovoka had inherited his zeal from his father, Tavibo, a self-proclaimed holy man who preached the return of the dead Indians and buffalo. When his father died, the fourteen-year-old Wovoka was adopted by a white ranching family who considered him their son, and the family's children thought of him as their brother. Wovoka was attentive to the Christian practices and nightly Bible reading by the couple.

The interchange between Wovoka and bystanders added more to Wovoka's story, and Winona translated. At age thirty, Wovoka said, he died and went to heaven where he met God who gave him instructions about the dance that would lead to salvation for the Indian people. Brett almost smiled when he recognized the influence of the adoptive parents' religion on the young Wovoka.

Winona described the story Wovoka told about an incident when he talked with some Paiutes who were skeptical about his claims of being blessed by God. He told the doubters that he would prove his powers by making ice appear in a nearby river on a certain day in July. When the ice indeed appeared as predicted, Wovoka's claims and his reputation were accepted.

Brett nodded, resisted the temptation to smile and to tell Winona the end of the story, which Wovoka did not tell, indeed which he might not have known. Brett recalled reading in a history that Wovoka's adoptive brothers were fearful that Wovoka's claim to produce ice in mid-July could prove his undoing. So on the given day, they loaded chunks of ice from their father's ice house and dumped them in the river upstream from the site where Wovoka and the skeptics awaited the miracle. When the chunks floated by, all doubts vanished.

That memory aroused another recollection that had surprised him when he first read it while preparing a lecture in his other life. It seems that Wovoka, the prophet sent by God to resurrect the old Indian ways, had a materialistic streak. A white man, though skeptical about Wovoka's claim to be able to bring rain, nevertheless was so desperate he asked Wovoka to do it, if he could. Wovoka agreed, and it actually rained as predicted.

That it did rain as predicted nourished Wovoka's confidence, and he decided that he should be paid for his services. He asked a friend at the local Indian agency to help him draft a letter to President Harrison. The letter requested the President pay him a small salary. In return, Wovoka would keep the local Nevada populace informed on the latest news from heaven, and he would provide rain whenever needed. The friend had second thoughts about the letter and never posted it. He did not tell Wovoka that he had pocketed the letter. Wovoka was miffed that he never received a reply from the President.

Wovoka complained to another government representative that white men should pay for his rainmaking services. Not much, perhaps two dollars, or five, ten or twenty-five or fifty, whatever they could pay without hurting themselves. Brett could not recall whether there was any response to his entreaty.

Brett started when he realized that Winona was whispering in his ear the latest comment from Wovoka to the eager throng. Wovoka was describing the meaning of the dance to a Sioux woman who was a member of a party that had arrived only last evening.

Brett was only half listening. For the last half hour, he had glanced repeatedly at a man across the circle who stared at him, his face grim. Brett would turn away, listening to Winona or looking at others in the throng, but he was pulled back to the man who continued to stare, his face sullen, if not angry.

Wovoka finished, and the crowd broke up, wandering from the circle in all directions, some talking softly, most quiet, lost in their thoughts. Only one did not move, the man who had been staring at Brett for the past half hour. Suddenly he strode directly for Brett. When he was almost upon him, he shouted and shook a fist. Brett did not understand, but recognized the Sioux language.

Winona, who had been talking with some women at her side, looked up, frowning. The man shouted again in Brett's direction, shaking his fist. Winona said something to the man, soft and passive. The man exploded, shaking his fist at her. She walked quickly to him, speaking rapidly, angrily. The man stopped, his jaw hanging, surprised at Winona's response. He recovered and shouted, leaning in her face.

Brett considered stepping in, but decided that Winnie was better than holding her own. He almost smiled.

Winona leaned toward the man, now almost nose to nose. She shouted, waving a fist in his face, advancing on him. The man's face fell, and he stepped backward. She advanced on him again, still speaking loudly and waving a fist in his face. He frowned, stepped back again, turned and walked away, looking back over his shoulder.

The women beside Winona had watched the confrontation silently, surprised. Now they laughed and spoke all at once to her. She smiled, said something, and the women withdrew, chatting and laughing as they walked away, looking back over their shoulders at her.

Winnie, her face blank, turned to Brett. "Whoa," he said softly. "My sweetheart is a warrior. What was that all about?"

"You."

"Me? How so?"

"He say you are a white man, and all white men bad,

do bad things to Indians. Everything that is bad for Indians today is because of white men. I tell him you are good white man. He say all white men bad. I say 'no.' I ask him if all Indians are good. He think about it and say, 'no, some Indians are bad.' I say, okay, some Indians good, some bad. Okay, some white men bad, some good. He don't like it, but he stop and walk away. I don't think he cause trouble."

Winona and Brett walked from the dance circle toward their camp. They stopped when an Indian walked toward them, calling, speaking in Sioux. He caught up and talked with Winona. He nodded abruptly to Brett and walked away. Brett and Winona continued walking toward their camp.

"You remember the man who said he is from village where Sitting Bull is?" she said. Brett nodded. "He say he and some others leave today and go to that village. He ask us go with them. He say Sitting Bull be glad to see us."

Brett continued walking, head down, and did not respond.

"Honey Brett?"

He looked aside at her. "That may not be a good idea."

She hesitated, frowning. "I think you know something." They continued walking. She looked at him again.

"Honey Brett?"

"You said you didn't want me to tell you if I knew something." She looked at him, frowning, and said no more.

They arrived at their camp. Brett picked up his reins and saddle from the ground and went to his horse.

He bridled the horse and threw the saddle onto the horse's back.

"Can we go?" she said. "I do what you say."

He leaned on his horse, staring over the horse's back into the distant plain. He turned to Winona. "I don't think you will be content unless we do. I will remind you that you said you will do what I say."

She went to him and hugged him, her head against his chest. "I am so happy to be with you, honey sweetheart, but I don't want to know. Too many bad things happen to Indian people, but I still hope." She took his face in her hands and kissed his lips. He watched her go to their bed and roll up the blankets.

Am I kind to her by letting her have her way, or should I tell her now? I'm just postponing her grief. God in heaven, if you're up there, if everything that happens is your will, why do you do this to these poor people?

They finished saddling their horses and loading the packhorse. They mounted, and Winona led the way to the meeting place with the Sioux who had invited them to go to their village. They joined a party of six, four men and two women. The men were well mounted; the women rode old horses that were better suited to transporting lodge poles and covers.

———

At dusk of the second day's ride, they camped beside the trail with a small party of Cheyenne who had ridden from the dancing ground only hours before the Sioux band left. The Cheyenne invited the Sioux to join them for feasting on an antelope they killed just before stopping. Chunks of meat roasted on spits over two campfires.

While Brett tended to the horses, Winona went to the fire and talked with the Cheyenne. The men spoke softly, watching the women at the cooking fires. The more they talked with Winona, the more animated they became, wide-eyed, faces contorted. A man jumped up and acted out something, jumping and whirling. Another joined in, bouncing up and down and singing to the heavens. Both men soon calmed and sat down at the fire, staring into the flames, contemplative.

Brett understood neither the pantomime nor the words. He had watched Winona during the performance, nodding slightly, leaning forward, caught up in the story. When it was finished, she came to him.

"You hear them?" she said. He nodded. "Yesterday, at beginning of night, just before they go to bed, they hear something outside camp. They look into dark between rows of trees, and they see small light coming. They watch, and the light grows, and the light becomes people, dead people from their tribe. They recognize the light people as their family and their friends. They visit with them, talk with them. Then the light people walk away, and they melt into darkness. They say this is what Wovoka said would happen."

Interesting. I can understand if one person hallucinates, but half a dozen? Simultaneously?

"That not all," Winona said. "This morning, early, before sun is high, they are on trail and they see herd of many buffalo. They kill one, and they cook it and eat it right there. They remember what Wovoka say so they leave the head, hoofs and tail where they kill it. Before they leave camp, the things they leave change to a live buffalo, and it run off. Other people say they see the new buffalo run away."

Hmm. Somebody a lot smarter—or crazier—than I will need to explain this to me.

"What you think?" said Winona.

He shook his head. "I don't know what to say, Winnie. Many people believe they saw their dead friends and relatives, and they believe they saw dead buffalo parts become a live buffalo. I can't explain it."

"But do you believe what they say?"

He paused. "I believe they think they saw what they say they saw."

She frowned, took his lapels and leaned her head against his chest, spoke softly into the folds of his shirt. "I don't understand what you say, but I think you say you don't believe them."

He took her head in his hands, pulled her face up to his. "Sweetheart, there are many things in heaven and Earth that I do not understand. But I try, and I do not judge anyone for believing something that I do not understand or believe." He kissed her forehead.

"Okay, I not sure I understand, but okay. Let's go to bed. That something I understand."

CHAPTER 9

High noon. Brett and Winona rode behind their Cheyenne and Sioux companions. The leader of the group told Winona they would arrive at the agency the next day. She rode up beside the leader and carried on a spirited conversation with him. Brett understood little, but heard the mention of Sitting Bull a number of times.

Sitting Bull. That would be at the Standing Rock Agency. Oh, how I wish I could check Google for the date. Today must be around December 13, 14? Is it time to take Winnie away? She wouldn't hear of it. She wants to see Sitting Bull. How can I permit that? If only I knew the date!

He strained, clenched his face, trying to resurrect the story. The Sioux had heard stories of Indian messiahs before, and they were skeptical when they first heard of the Paiute prophet, Wovoka. But the more they heard, the more they wondered. After all, if the followers of the Christian god believed fervently in the existence of a messiah, why not an Indian messiah?

Even Red Cloud at Pine Ridge Agency, now a Catholic, began to wonder.

The Sioux chiefs had sent a delegation to Nevada to investigate the claims of this self-proclaimed messiah. The party traveled west by train and horse, visiting with other tribes along the way and mixing with them at the gathering in Nevada.

When they returned to the Dakota agencies, the delegation's report was enthusiastic, but they tailored the messiah's message to their own needs. They ignored Wovoka's urging to farm and work alongside whites and to send their children to schools and to live at peace with whites. Instead, they interpreted his message to promise the end of white domination of Indians. Assuming this policy could mean conflict with whites, militant leaders introduced the ghost shirt. Wear this shirt, they said, and bullets cannot hurt you. They cannot penetrate the shirt.

General Nelson Miles, the local military commander, believed that Sitting Bull was encouraging the Ghost Dancers to the extent that all other activity at the agency seemed at a standstill. Miles decided to arrest him and transport him to a military prison. He knew he would have to tread lightly due to Sitting Bull's position among the Sioux. He was still revered as a chief and spiritual leader.

In early November, General Miles asked William F. Cody to persuade Sitting Bull to give himself up. He was aware that Cody knew Sitting Bull well since the chief had appeared in Cody's Wild West Show. Cody agreed to the plan, though it is unclear whether he was told that the chief was to be sent to a military prison.

By the time Cody arrived at the agency in late

November, James McLaughlin, the agent at Standing Rock, had heard of the plan and called it off. If there were to be an arrest, said McLaughlin, it would be made by his own Indian police officers. He reasoned that there would be less problem with this plan than involving the army. On the other hand, maybe he would just wait for cold weather, and the Indians would be forced to wait out the winter in quarters at the agency.

What is the date? Where are we in this scenario? Brett closed his eyes and shook his head, looking up into the cloudless sky. *I am haunted, bewitched, abandoned. Am I going to survive this cursed transportation?* He looked at Winona ahead, still riding beside the leader, talking with him, a smile playing about her lips. He looked into the heavens, his eyes closed.

A rider ahead on the trail approached at a gallop. He pulled up beside the leader. The rider spoke rapidly, excited. Winona leaned forward, listening. The leader finally nodded, and the rider joined the others. Winona pulled back beside Brett.

"What was he so excited about?" said Brett.

"I don't understand. He say somebody name Cody come to agency, ask to see Sitting Bull. Agent name McLaughlin say 'no'."

Brett frowned. *Cody. It's happening, exactly as I have read in the histories. I feel I'm watching a movie I've already seen, a movie I don't want to see. I wish I could take Winnie and ride away from here, go some-place that the history books never mentioned.* He shook his head. *I would have to tie and gag her to do that. She wants to see Sitting Bull.*

Brett closed his eyes, trying to remember what comes next. McLaughlin decides that he has to act. In mid-December, he assembles forty-three native police to make the arrest. In coordination, the army commander stations a force of a hundred troopers and a Hotchkiss gun in the vicinity as backup.

Brett grimaced. *When does all this happen? Today? Tomorrow?*

———

Brett moved about the campground at first light. He was first up and made no attempt to be quiet. He collected firewood, went to the firepit, held the sticks high and dropped them beside the firepit. He cleared his throat noisily, hummed a tune, coughed.

Winona raised up, frowning at him. "Be quiet," she whispered.

He bent over her, whispered, "We need to move! We need to reach Standing Rock soon as possible. Things may happen there today."

She looked blankly, then seemed to comprehend. Crawling from bed, she rolled the blankets. Brett dragged saddles and bridles to the hobbled horses and set to work on them. One by one, the Cheyenne awoke, frowning, but rose and began preparing for departure.

———

The band rode slowly on the trail toward Standing Rock Agency. They saw a small party of horsemen ahead by the trail, reined up and the leader spoke with them.

Brett stared at a man in the party who did not seem to fit. He was white, dressed in buckskins and tassels, but these were not Indian buckskins. They were tailored and colored. The man sported a mustache and goatee.

Yes! It's him! William F. Cody, Buffalo Bill.

Cody stared at Brett. He had spotted this white man at the same time that Brett recognized him.

"You're not of this tribe, I think," said Cody, smiling.

Brett rode to him, glancing aside at Winona who looked at him, a question on her face.

"Mr. Cody. I have seen your pictures."

Cody smiled. "How do you happen to be in Dakota at this perilous moment?"

Brett hesitated. *Who am I at this perilous moment, and why am I here?* "Uh...Brett Davis, *Dallas Morning News.* Trying to give my readers a close-up account of what's happening with the Sioux people. I wonder whether you can tell me something of what you are doing here. I'm aware that you are a friend of Sitting Bull."

"*Dallas Morning News?* I don't know it. As a matter of fact, I had a few newsmen accompanying me until they decided I was no longer news and hightailed it. As for Sitting Bull, you'll know about our association. General Miles also knows about my friendship with Sitting Bull. The general and other authorities believe that Sitting Bull is going to encourage the Ghost Dance at Standing Rock. They wanted me to persuade the chief that he should give it up and surrender peacefully to the local army commander. So I load up a wagon with sweets—the chief loves sweets—and proceed to Standing Rock.

"I had no sooner arrived at the agency than Major

McLaughlin, the agent, blew his top." Cody smiled. "Uh, you will use your judgment with the language you put in your story, I trust." Brett nodded.

"McLaughlin said that I was not to see Sitting Bull under any circumstances. He said he would take care of the chief in his own time and his own fashion. He was convinced that Sitting Bull was about to rouse his people to do the Ghost Dance and prepare for the coming of the new world. And McLaughlin added, a bit pompously, I thought, that he had received word that President Harrison had told General Miles that I was not to interfere with local authorities.

"Well, I talked with a friend of the chief, my friend also, you understand. This man was with Sitting Bull when the chief was a member of my show. Anyway, this friend said that he had talked with some of Sitting Bull's people, and they said that the chief was preparing to go to Pine Ridge Agency. It seems Sitting Bull had been told that God was going to appear at Pine Ridge, and he didn't want to miss this. When agent McLaughlin heard about this plan, my friend said, he exploded.

"So here I am, heading north for the railway station at Mandan where I will catch the first train for home. If you are here to deal with the situation, I wish you luck." He waved a goodbye and set off with his companions.

Brett watched him go. As Cody's party rode slowly in single file on the narrow trail, Brett pondered. *Wow. I have just had a conversation with William F. Buffalo Bill Cody. We talked about Sitting Bull who I will likely see again shortly. What will I say to my students about this meeting?* He looked aside. *Will I ever stand before a room of students again? If I do, will my memory be intact, or will it be wiped clean? Hmm. That's a possibility. Hadn't thought about that.*

"Are you okay, honey?" said Winona. He looked aside at her, his face blank. "Brett?"

"I'm okay. Let's catch up." He kicked his horse to a slow lope toward their companions who had ridden ahead when Brett and Winona stopped to talk with Cody.

————

The Sioux party that included Brett and Winona rode into the outskirts of Standing Rock Agency. As a professor of western history, Brett had always been interested in the institution of the Indian agency, the government replacement for the Indian village. He could never decide whether the agency was a vehicle for ushering native Americans into the modern age, or a prison without walls.

Now, he had a first-hand look at an important agency. He saw log cabins, no lodges. He had been told by others in the party that the agency included a store, a post office and the beginnings of a school and church. He saw no evidence of these harbingers of white man's civilization. Perhaps they were further into the agency properties. He understood there would also be government buildings where provisions were housed and dispensed, but he saw none of these.

They passed men and women who stepped off the trail to watch the strangers come. The people wore a combination of ragged Indian dress and white people's clothing, shabby and castoff.

Brett looked around for any indication of what the

histories said was about to happen. He saw a sizable group of men ahead across a clearing, standing and sitting in the shade of a cluster of trees. They smoked and gestured as they talked. Brett squinted. They appeared to wear uniforms. Indian men wearing uniforms. Indian police.

Beyond the police, a small detachment of troopers, a couple of dozen perhaps, sat their horses in a sunny opening in the woods. The horses moved about, troopers pulling them back into a tight formation. The troopers watched Brett and Winona's party approach.

All according to the written record so far.

The leader of the party reined up, hailing a couple of men walking just off the trail. The walkers stopped. At the leader's question, one pointed to a house off the trail. The rider turned and looked at the house. He said something more to the walkers who went on their way.

Winona leaned toward Brett, pulled on his sleeve and spoke softly. "They say that house belong Sitting Bull!" She pointed. "They say he there now. Cheyenne leader going there now, and he ask if we want go. I say 'yes'. Okay?"

Brett looked at the house. A half dozen men stood in the yard, chatting. He stared at the house, frowning.

"Brett honey? Okay? I want see him."

Brett looked at the group of uniformed men at the trees. They stood and sat, passing the time. He heard laughter.

"Okay," said Brett. "Let's be quick. Come on." He kicked his horse to a lope toward the house. Winona, surprised, kicked her horse and followed.

They pulled up in front of the house. Some Indian men lounged in the yard, smoking, chatting. Three men stood at the door. All watched Brett and Winona dismount.

"You go on," said Brett. "I'll take care of the horses and come over." She stood where she dismounted, waiting. "Go on, Winnie. Go inside and see him. I'll be right there." *Why am I doing this?* Winona still stood, waiting. "Winnie, do you hear me?" he said sharply. "Go now, talk with Sitting Bull, if that's what you want to do. I'll tie the horses and be right there."

She winced at his sharp tone, turned and walked to the house.

He led the horses to a tree thirty yards from the house and tied the reins to a low limb. He looked across the flat toward the police. They had not moved from their position at the grove. A dozen more uniformed men had joined them, and they chatted, some laughing lightly. But Brett sensed a subdued tension, as most of them looked toward Sitting Bull's house. And at him.

He strode, almost running, toward the house. He raised a hand in greeting to the men who stood outside the door. They frowned at this white man but stepped aside. *I suppose they noticed that I rode in with Winnie. They might remember her from the dance. At least, they would have noticed that she is Indian and seemed to know what she was doing.*

Brett stepped through the open door into the house. Winona stood beside a seated Sitting Bull. They talked amicably, Winona leaning toward him, he staring at the floor and door, nodding occasionally, almost smiling. Brett held up a hand in greeting. Sitting Bull looked up, nodded, and raised a hand in recognition. The chief repeatedly glanced at the door.

Brett also watched the door. He started. Through

the opening, he saw that the Indian Police had left their sheltered place at the trees and now walked slowly, directly toward the house. The scattered Indians near the house saw the police coming and began walking toward the house, glancing back at the approaching police.

Brett went to Winona, leaned down and whispered into her ear, "We need to leave now, right now, quickly. Say goodbye."

She straightened, frowned at him. "We just got here. I want talk to him."

Brett looked through the door. The police still walked toward the house, following the leader. *That would be... Bull Head.* They were almost in the yard. *There must be three dozen or more now.* He whispered, sharply, "Winnie! We must go now." He grasped her arm tightly and pulled her toward the door. She frowned and tried to pull away.

A sharper whisper than before: "Winnie! You said you would do what I say! Remember?"

She relaxed, stood, and walked with him to the door. She stopped in the doorway, looked back to Sitting Bull. He looked up at her, nodded once, looked down.

Still holding her arm, Brett pulled her outside. They saw the police, now almost to the house. Winnie stopped, looked up at Brett, her face a question.

Brett tightened his hold on her arm. They stepped away from the door only a moment before the police arrived. A scattering of people had followed the police as they approached the house, and now a throng of at least a hundred angry men stood in the yard, some grumbling, some shouting and waving fists.

Most of the police stopped at the door, only Bull Head and two others going into the house. The police who remained outside turned to face the men in the yard.

Brett led Winona toward the horses, still tightly holding her arm. She looked over her shoulder toward the house as Brett strode ahead, head down.

They stopped beside the horses. She turned back to look at the house, trying to pull away, but he still held her.

She relaxed. "Okay, I stay," she said softly. She put a hand on his until he released her.

They watched the house. "You know, don't you?" she said softly. He stared at the house and the crowd of police and others in the yard.

Brett and Winona heard loud voices from inside the house. Bull Head stepped from inside to the doorway and said something loudly to the police outside.

"He say Sitting Bull under arrest, coming out," Winona said.

A policeman led Sitting Bull's horse close to the door of the cabin. Sensing what was about to happen, the crowd in the yard surged forward. They shouted and shook fists at the police.

Winona translated quickly in bits, straining to hear. "A man say 'kill them! Shoot police!' Another man say 'do what agent say. Go with police'. A woman—I think she Sitting Bull wife we see at Little Big Horn village— she sing:

> *Sitting Bull*
> *You have always been*
> *A brave man*

What is going
To happen now?

"Another man say 'brother, let us go to agency together. You take your family. I take mine. If you are to die there, I die with you'."

Sitting Bull suddenly appeared in the doorway between Bull Head and another policeman.

The men in the yard shouted louder and surged toward the house. Then a young man yelled something above the din.

Winona looked at Brett, wide-eyed. "He call Sitting Bull coward, tell him stay, not come out, not give up." Sitting Bull heard this, stopped, pulled back, yelling to the crowd.

Winona pressed her hands on her cheeks. "He ask followers to rescue him!" she said.

Suddenly a shot rang out from the mob. Bull Head at the doorway grabbed his side. He brought his pistol up, seemingly to fire at his assailant, but shot Sitting Bull in the chest as he fell. The policeman standing behind Sitting Bull raised his pistol quickly and shot the chief in the back of the head. Sitting Bull collapsed to the ground.

The crowd, hugely outnumbering the police, erupted and attacked the police with clubs, knives and guns. But the police were a formidable force, trained and better armed, and they held their ground. The crowd in the yard turned at the sound of galloping horses and saw troopers bearing down on them. The mob, grumbling, yelling and shaking fists, withdrew slowly, turning occasionally to shout threats at the police and soldiers.

Throughout the melee of shots and shouts, Sitting Bull's circus horse performed as he had performed in Cody's Wild West show. He sat on his haunches, lifting his forehooves as if in prayer.

————

Dusk. Winnie and Brett sat before a small fire on the outskirts of Standing Rock. Their three horses were hobbled nearby. They stared at squirrel and rabbit carcasses, skewered on a stick, roasting over the fire. Juices from the meat dripped on the embers, causing tiny eruptions of flames.

"You eat rabbit; I eat squirrel," she said, without looking at him.

He smiled thinly. "One of these days when you're real hungry, I'm going to shoot a dozen rabbits and nothing else and see what you'll do."

"I eat it, but if I sick, it your fault."

They watched the cooking in silence. Eventually she lifted the stick and laid it on a couple of flat stones she had collected earlier and cleaned off for their makeshift table. She pushed the carcasses off the stick, placing the rabbit before Brett and took the squirrel for herself.

She pulled off a small chunk and tasted, wrinkling her nose. "I don't like squirrel," she said, "but I don't like rabbit more than squirrel."

They ate in silence, pulling slivers of meat from the bones, shaking a hand when the hot meat burned. When she finished, she started to drop the squirrel carcass on the flames, but Brett took it from her and placed it on the rock before him. He tossed the clean rabbit bones on the flames and worked on the squirrel. She glanced at him blankly, then stared into the flames. Shortly he dropped the squirrel bones on the fire and wiped his hands on grass.

She moved over to him and leaned on his shoulder. They watched the western horizon darken as the memory of the sunset dimmed. The filmy cloud layer at the horizon changed color from magenta to pink to gray and disappeared. He stirred the fire with a stick and dropped it on the dying embers. The dry stick burst into flame and burned out as the embers were reduced to a faint glow.

"I'll get some more tinder so we can keep it burning," he said. "Likely to cool down tonight."

She stared into the embers, then turned to him. "Brett?"

"Winnie?"

"I think if I knew what was going to happen, I would try do something."

He clenched his jaw. "I know it's hard to understand, sweetheart, and even harder to accept. But nothing I could have done was going to change what was going to happen. I have read in books that agency police kill Sitting Bull in his own house. And that's what happened. I could not change that, no matter what I tried to do. If I had tried to do something, likely I would have been killed, and no history book would record my death." He shook his head, spoke softly. "I don't exist in history, not this history."

She looked at him, her face drawn. When he did not respond, she turned back and stared into the embers, rocking back and forth. She wiped a single tear from her cheek with the back of a hand. "I know. I know. But... it all so hard to understand. I think my head gonna break."

Brett put an arm around her shoulders and pulled her close. She leaned her head on his arm. "I don't understand either," he said, "I just know."

"It so sad. He was good man, good leader of Indian people. I think white people would like to kill all Indian people. Then troubles would stop. Then Indian people would cause no trouble, and all Indian land would be white man land."

"All white people?" he said. "Me?"

She took his hand and kissed it. "No, not you, honey, not you."

"There are many good white people who believe that Indian people have not been treated fairly. However, these people mostly live in towns far from Indian country. These are not people who would like to take Indian land so they can farm it. It's easy to believe in something if it doesn't affect your pocketbook."

She leaned on his shoulder. "I don't know 'pocketbook', but I think I understand." She stood. "I go get wood. I understand warm and cold."

She took two steps, stopped, looked down a long moment. She turned. "I don't think I could live in your time. No Indian people there. Only ghosts."

———

Brett awoke at first light, shivering. He pulled the blanket to his chin, still shivering. He pushed the blanket down, reached for his coat and struggled into it. He pulled on his boots, went to the fire circle, and knelt at the stones. Stirring ashes in the firepit, he finally saw the glow of a few embers. He dropped small dry sticks on the embers until they caught, then lay larger dry boughs on the flames.

Warming his hands over the flames, he jerked aside when something soft fell from above on his shoulder and arms. He looked up to see snow on pine boughs above him.

"Brett." He turned to see Winona, peering from under the blanket which she held at her neck. "It so cold."

"Come to the fire. Bring the blanket with you."

She sat up and stood, went quickly to the fire and sat beside Brett, holding the blanket tight around her shoulders. She frowned, looked across the flames at the ground, turned abruptly to Brett. "Snow?"

"Appears so."

"Honey. I don't understand."

I have given up trying to understand. But at least I know what is happening.

"Winnie, sweetheart, I think we have been transported. I don't know where. We will find out soon enough, I suppose. The important thing, for me, is that you are with me."

They dressed and broke camp without breakfast, agreeing that they would find a sunny trail and worry about eating later. They rode south on a trail that ran parallel to the banks of a narrow stream. Tall grasses at water's edge glistened with snow crystals that had begun to melt.

"Where we go now?" Winona said.

He frowned, eyes closed, swaying with the rhythm of the walking horse.

"Honey?" she said.

He opened his eyes, looked at her. "I don't know. Some cosmic force is going to guide us somewhere. We have no choice."

"Why we have no choice? We knew we go to Abilene. We knew we go Standing Rock."

He pondered, glanced aside at her. "That's true. We knew we wanted to go to those places. We had purpose when we went to those places. I sense no purpose now. Our horses probably know better than we where we are going."

"What is 'cos-mic force'?"

He smiled faintly, staring at his saddle horn. "I knew you were going to ask that when I said it." He looked up into the scudding gray clouds in the blue sky. "Cosmic force. Hmm. It is something beyond our understanding. Something we don't know, something we can't explain."

She watched him a moment, frowning. "Honey, sometimes you strange."

He smiled a hint of a smile. "Yeah, I know."

They rode on a faint trail, lightly marked with deer and horse hooves and droppings, bordered by patches of fresh snow. Brett was lost in thought, wondering about the meaning of what he had experienced in these past weeks, or was it months? Or years? He simply could find no meaning or explanation. *Am I supposed to be learning something from all this? If so, then what?*

Morning gave way to afternoon as they rode silently. Occasionally Winona glanced aside at Brett and started to speak but was dissuaded by his grim face.

They rode around a thick stand of pines, and Brett abruptly reined up. He held out a hand to signal a stop. They saw ahead a cluster of lodges near the banks of a river. In the center of the village, dozens of men and women, holding hands and knees bent, shuffled sideways in a circle, singing and following the cadence of drums. The Ghost Dance.

Here's that cosmic force again. We have ridden, I think, less than a hundred miles from Standing Rock Agency. I fear I know more about this village than I want to know.

Brett and Winona rode slowly into the camp. A few of the people they passed stopped to watch the two strangers. Some seemed to nod in recognition. Winona spoke to three women briefly as they passed, and one of the women responded.

When they had ridden past, Winona turned to him. "I remember them," she said softly to Brett. "They were at Sitting Bull's camp on Bighorn River. I talk with them at that camp." One of the women left the others and hurried, almost running, to the center of the village.

Riding into the heart of the village, they were intercepted by a man striding to them. He spoke to Winona, then waited.

"He say Chief Hump want talk with us," she said. "We go with him. Okay?" Brett nodded. She spoke with the man, and he turned and walked briskly ahead. Brett and Winona walked their horses after him.

Yes, as I suspected. The river over there would be the Cheyenne River, and that would be the village of Chief Hump. Oh, my. I know where this is going. Damn cosmic force.

Gad, if I only had one good history book, I wouldn't be challenging my brain power every time I need to dredge up an episode.

He recalled that many of the followers of Sitting

Bull who scattered after the chief's death fled to Hump's camp in the south at the mouth of Cherry Creek on the Cheyenne River. There they joined friends and relations who had been doing the Ghost Dance for weeks. The newcomers eagerly joined the dance, desperately seeking salvation in the midst of chaos.

Brett and Winona reined up where the messenger spoke to a man Brett assumed to be Chief Hump. He didn't recall having seen pictures of Hump. They dismounted as Hump spoke to Winnie. She listened, translated, waited for Brett's acknowledgement, and translated again.

The gist of the conversation was that the chief had learned that the nearest civil authorities were alarmed by the dancing in Hump's village and thought him a dangerous leader who was preparing his people for trouble of some sort. The authorities were particularly concerned that Hump had welcomed some of Sitting Bull's followers after they fled Standing Rock. The authorities knew many of them were still angry and Hump's taking them in was ominous. Furthermore, Hump's village, augmented by the discontented followers of Sitting Bull, continued to practice the Ghost Dance.

When contacted by authorities, Hump assured them that he had no hostile intentions. His people were peaceful and hungry, he said, and only danced in the hope that the old ways could come back. Peacefully, he repeated.

Hump spoke to Winona in Sioux, and she translated. "He say he very glad to see us here. He say a follower of Sitting Bull say we are good people. He ask us to help him. He say he just today receive letter that say an old army friend name Captain Ewers coming to see him. He want us go with him and help convince Captain that his people are peaceful and do not have bad hearts. He ask if we can help."

Brett listened to Winona, nodding as she translated. "Yes, we will go with him," Brett said, "and do what we can." Winona translated. The chief took Brett's hand in both of his and shook it.

Hump spoke to Winona, and she translated as the chief and his companion walked away. "He say we leave tomorrow early."

CHAPTER 10

Sunrise. Golden rays flowed through the leafless oaks on both sides of the trail. Winona and Brett rode behind Hump and a companion, Brett leading their packhorse. He looked up suddenly at the chirping whistle of a western meadowlark but could not find the singer. His eyes clouded. He marveled that, in the midst of suffering and chaos, he could still be captivated by birdsong.

There was little conversation during the days on the trail, but evenings around the campfire Hump described the desperate condition of the people in his village. These poor people, hungry and almost naked, he said, had witnessed so much tragedy lately that the Ghost Dance seemed their only hope. They knew of Sitting Bull's death and the scattering of his followers. They feared something as tragic could happen to them and despaired of any change in their condition. They danced out of desperation, a last hope for salvation. The arrival of some of Sitting Bull's followers added a measure of anger to the suffering of Bull's people.

On the fourth day on the trail, at high noon they saw two uniformed riders ahead. Hump yelled and kicked his horse into a gallop toward the men. Brett and Winona, surprised, galloped after him.

The two soldiers saw the three riders approaching. The soldiers dismounted and waited. Hump reined up and slid from the saddle. He strode to the captain and extended his hand. Winona and Brett dismounted, stood behind Hump.

"Captain Ewers, my friend!" Hump said.

Ewers shook the hand, turned to his companion. "This is Lieutenant Willis."

Hump pumped Willis's hand quickly, introduced Brett and Winona as quickly, and turned to Ewers, smiling. The old friends spoke animatedly in a mishmash of Sioux and English. They talked about old times when Captain Ewers was the officer assigned to conduct affairs between Hump and the various agency and army authorities. The two had become good friends, and Hump trusted him.

Now Ewers explained that some officials were concerned that Hump's people were actively performing the Ghost Dance and that some of Sitting Bull's followers had recently appeared in his village. They feared that Hump might be in danger of being influenced by bad people.

"The authorities have asked me to persuade you to take your people to Fort Bennett on the Missouri River," said Ewers, "where they will be safe from influence of these bad people, these hostiles that could cause trouble."

"Captain, my old friend, I will do anything you ask. I trust you." They walked toward their tethered mounts, chatting amicably, laughing. Hump clapped Ewers on the back. The Lieutenant looked at Brett, smiled, and followed Hump and Ewers, leading his horse.

Brett and Winona watched them go. She frowned, turned to Brett. "Strange," she said. She waited, but Brett said nothing. "You know about this, don't you?" He nodded. "I sometime forget you know about everything we see and what is going to happen."

"Not everything, sweetheart. Just what I read in books. The books don't tell everything."

"Does Hump take his people to Fort Bennett?"

"Oh, yes. They all go to Bennett."

"Does Hump do what Captain wants him to do?"

"Yes, as well as he can. Hump even becomes a scout for the army and persuades some of Sitting Bull's people, who are still angry, not to join the hostiles in the wild country called the Badlands."

"How will Hump's people like Fort Bennett? Will they be happy there?"

Brett looked up, pondering. "I don't recall reading much about how they fare at the fort. I do remember they stop dancing and become dependent on the army and agents. They probably will be as hungry and ragged there as they were at Hump's village.

"We should not go to Fort Bennett," he said. "These people have lost the old ways, moving about whenever they wished, going anywhere they wished. Now they will live in one place inside the four walls of wooden houses, receiving their food from government storehouses. It will not be a happy place."

"I don't want go there," she said. "Will you tell Chief Hump we not going back to village with him?"

"Yes. There's nothing more to be done here."

Brett mounted and rode to the copse where Hump and the soldiers stood beside their horses. He dismounted, waited for a break in the conversation, then spoke to Hump. The chief nodded, said his thanks, to which Brett wished him good luck. Brett shook hands with the soldiers, mounted and rode back to Winona.

They sat their horses in silence, watching the three still standing beside their mounts, talking and gesturing, occasionally laughing. Hump's pleasure in resuming an old friendship was obvious.

"Honey Brett?"

"Winnie sweetheart?'

"Can we go somewhere you don't know? Maybe someplace I know better than you? Or someplace you or me don't know? Maybe some place you never see, even in books? And we meet people you never see in books?"

He reached over and took her hand. "I would like that. Heaven knows I would like that. We'll try. But— you remember when I said some cosmic force decides where we are going and what we see? I don't know how it works, but that cosmic force likely will decide where we go next. We can set out in any direction, and likely we will be led to whatever place or event that we are destined to see. Does that make sense?"

"No. I understand what you say, but I not understand why we cannot go somewhere we want to go and not where this cos-thing tell us to go."

"Good point. How's this? You decide which direction to ride, and we'll go that way and see what we find. As long as we can find game along the way and don't run into bad people, we'll go where you want to go. Sound okay?"

"Yes."

"Lead off. I'll follow you. You find the trail, and I'll watch for supper. Should be able to scare up a few rabbits in this meadow."

She wrinkled her nose and set out on what appeared to be a faint game trail across a grassy flat. He reined in behind her and let her set the pace. He lagged a bit so she would not be pressured by a close follower.

They rode slowly under a clear, cold sky. He looked with some concern at a dark line of clouds above the western horizon that had been creeping their way since noon. They hadn't had to use the oiled canvas since a wet day on the Little Bighorn, but by evening they might need to set it up.

The Little Bighorn. It seems a lifetime ago. Has it been years in my life? 1876 to 1890. Have I aged, let's see, fourteen years since then? Winnie certainly hasn't aged fourteen years. Every morning when she first opens her eyes and kisses me, she seems a year younger than yesterday. Oh, how I love that sweet woman! If I didn't have her with me on this strange trip, I think I would have shot myself.

He squinted at what he thought was movement at the edge of a wood ahead. "Winnie," he whispered, just loud enough for her to hear. She looked at him over her shoulder. "Do you see animals at the edge of the trees ahead, left of the trail?"

She looked. "Yes, three or four deer. They see us."

"You keep riding on the trail, same pace. I'm giving you the pack horse reins. I'm moving left for a better shot." He rode up beside her, handed her the reins, then turned slightly leftward and moved slowly through the tall grass.

Upon reaching the line of pine trees, he rode slowly

in the dark shade. The three deer saw him, but focused more on Winona and the packhorse. He reined up under a limb, dismounted, and tied the reins to the limb. Drawing the rifle slowly from its scabbard—*no quick movements, pard*—he walked a few steps away from the horse, steadied himself, aimed, and fired. The deer bolted, and one collapsed after but a few steps.

He slid the rifle into the scabbard, mounted, and loped to the downed deer. He reined up beside the carcass, dismounted, and tied the reins to a pine sapling. He stood, watching Winona till she reined up beside his horse. She dismounted and tied the reins of the two horses beside his. She walked to him, kissed his cheek.

"Good shot. Why you stand there, watching me?"

"Well... uh."

"I gonna teach you to cut up deer. What you do if I not here? Look at dead deer and hope somebody come by to cut up deer for you?"

He took her cheeks in his hands. "Don't even joke about that. You will always be here. With me. If you are not, I'll shoot myself."

She pulled his hands down roughly. "You keep saying that! Don't you say that! Don't!" She put her arms around his neck and rested her head against his chest. "Don't. Not funny," she said softly.

"I'm sorry, sweetheart. I guess I'm just saying I don't know what I would do without you."

"Okay." She pushed him away, went to her mount, opened a saddlebag and took out a sheathed knife. Pulling the knife from the sheath, she showed it to him. "Watch. I teach you." She knelt beside the deer carcass and began to cut.

―――――

The cooking fire softly illuminated the canopy of nearby trees and the three horses hobbled under them. Winona and Brett sat at the fire circle, eating slices of roasted venison. A small chunk of meat remained on the spit.

The deer carcass hung from a tree limb near the hobbled horses. He had strung up the deer at eye level, not noticing Winona's frown. She told him to hang it higher, out of reach of bears. He listened carefully, took the deer down, and hung it from a tree a good distance from the campfire. She agreed that was a good idea since they didn't want to attract bears to their camp.

Winona wiped her hands on the grass. "That was good. I glad you good shot." She glanced aside at him. "Next time you cut up deer. Okay?"

He smiled. "I'll shoot a rabbit next time, and I'll cut it up." She frowned, punched his arm as he winced.

They sat silently, staring into the fire. Brett looked toward the west, saw nothing but darkness. The black cloud had moved overhead by sunset, and he stretched the canvas, expecting wet weather.

He looked at the small piece of venison on the spit, calculating whether he could hold even that small bit in his full belly. "Winnie, would you like——"

"Brett," softly.

He turned to her, followed her stare into the darkness. "What is it, honey?"

"Somebody there."

He looked again at the darkness and saw what appeared to be the dark outline of a person. As his eyes became accustomed to the dark, another form took shape beside the first one, then another, and another.

Brett was startled when Winona said something in Sioux to the apparitions. A voice answered softly. Winona spoke again, and someone responded. Winona stood and walked toward the figures.

"Winnie." Brett stood and stepped toward Winona. "What are..." She waved him away, and he stopped.

Winona went to the figures and merged with the shadows. After a moment she walked back to the fire, a woman beside her, and a dozen more men and women and some children behind. A boy led two gaunt horses with packs.

"Honey, they hungry. She say they not eat in three days. I tell them we have food and come to camp."

"Good, Winnie, good." He pointed to the ground at the fire, guided a small girl and boy to the fire, showed them where to sit. Winona led two women to the hanging deer carcass. She lowered it and handed her knife to a woman. The second woman produced a knife from somewhere, and both began carving chunks from the deer. The others went to the fire, extended hands over the flames to warm themselves in the cold night, silently watched the carvers.

Meanwhile, both Brett and Winona fed the fire with sticks they had collected earlier for the nighttime fire. While one woman continued slicing the carcass, the other came to the fire, removed the small chunk from the spit, and handed it to a small boy. She pushed chunks of fresh meat on the spit and placed it on the forked sticks. Winona handed the woman another stick for roasting while Brett pushed forked sticks on each side of the firepit. Soon the two roasting sticks were filled with slices and chunks of venison.

The carcass soon was almost clean, and the people well fed. Winnie told them to spread their blankets around the fire. A man said this would be the first time they had been warm in many days. He started to tell her more, but Winnie said to sleep now, and they would talk in the morning. The people pulled thin blankets off the pack horses and laid them around the fire.

Winnie and Brett made their beds near their hobbled horses. She lay close, whispered, "They not hungry now, but they very sad. They talk to us tomorrow."

———

Brett and Winona awoke to the smell of roasting venison. Their visitors huddled around the fire over which small chunks of meat on a spit sputtered over the flames. He glanced at the hanging carcass and saw that it was clean.

Winona stood, pulling a blanket around her shoulders, and went to the fire. She sat and exchanged greetings with the women while Brett headed for the bushes behind camp. When he returned, he sat beside Winona, and she offered him a small slice of venison. She talked with the women and men in Sioux, gesturing occasionally at Brett.

When she finished eating, Winona spoke to Brett. "They from Sitting Bull's band. They leave agency after the trouble there. They not know what to do, where to go. But they hear some people from agency go to Chief Big Foot camp. They look for camp of Big Foot now."

Big Foot. Of course. This devil cosmic force decrees we go to Big Foot's camp. Why am I not surprised?

Winona waited for Brett to respond, but he said nothing, staring into the flames.

After a long moment, Winona took his hand, studied his face. "I think you know Big Foot."

He stared at the fire. "Yes, I know something of Big Foot."

She waited, but he said no more. "Do I want to know about Big Foot?" she said.

He searched the sky, deep clear blue with only a few wispy white clouds. The light rain during the night had ended before sunrise. "We will go with the people to Big Foot's camp. If I remember correctly, it's on the Cheyenne River, not too far from here, I think. I believe we'll see other Sitting Bull followers there. After the chief's murder at Standing Rock, his people scattered. Some went to Hump, some to Big Foot, and some simply to wander, their lives so disrupted they didn't know what to do or where to go."

"These people want go to Big Foot camp. Do we have to go there? Why not go other direction?"

He wrapped his arms about her shoulders, pulled her to him. "I feel compelled, sweetheart. You know I can't explain. If we went in another direction, we would still end up there. I can't explain it. Cosmic force."

She rubbed her face in the folds of his shirt. "Damn cosmic force," she said, softly.

He drew back, pulled a face, almost smiling. "Whoa, where did my little Cheyenne sweetheart learn white man's profanity?"

She ducked her head, smiling a hint of a smile. "From white man. Man I live with. He use bad language all time. His wife say: 'you say that; you go to hell.' He say, 'you go to hell, woman.' I think she not go to hell. She good woman. *He* go to hell. He bad man."

Brett kissed her forehead. "You good woman; you angel."

She frowned, spoke deliberately. "You *are a* good man. You *are a* angel."

He grabbed her and hugged her tightly. *What will become of me if the cursed cosmic force takes my angel?*

She leaned back, saw the single tear on his cheek. She wiped the tear and kissed his lips. "I love you, honey Brett." He hugged her again, looked over her shoulder to see the entire body of Sioux visitors staring at them. Winona pulled back and saw them. The people smiled, a woman said something to her, and everyone laughed. Winona thought a moment, then replied, and they laughed again.

The people stood, chatting, looking aside at Brett and Winona, laughing softly, as they went to their beds. They gathered their meager belongings and carried them to the two packhorses. While Brett worked at saddling their horses, Winnie rolled their blankets and stuffed them into the panniers. Done with saddling, he helped Winnie at the packhorse.

"What did the woman say to you?" he said.

"She say, 'I think you own him. How much he cost?' I say 'I bought him and my horse same time.' I say 'I pay more for horse'."

"Hmm. I guess that makes sense. I can't run as fast as your horse, and I can't carry as much stuff as your horse." They untied reins from the limb and mounted.

"They are better at walking than we are, but tell them if anyone needs to ride, we'll walk a while." She spoke to the group, and they nodded. A couple of women replied.

Brett led off that morning on a dim trail that he somehow reckoned would lead them to Big Foot's village. His reckoning was correct. *How could I go wrong when the cosmic force determines our path?* Near sundown on the second day, the group stood in the midst of what had been a village, now deserted, leaving only some castoff clothing, rags, and a few shredded blankets. Clear outlines of lodges and fire circles suggested a recent departure. The Indians muttered among themselves, confused and unsure what to do next.

Winona looked at Brett. He shook his head, strolled to their horses tied to a sapling. She went to the group, listened as they discussed their desperate situation. They had no food, few blankets, and some were almost naked. Then they brightened at what a man said and seemed to gather strength, perhaps hope.

Winona went to Brett. "A man said he thinks Big Foot's people receive their annuities at Pine Ridge Agency. He thinks they may be on the trail now, going to Pine Ridge."

Brett smiled. "That is a smart man."

She frowned. "You know. Why you not tell them.?"

"They would think me a prophet and look to me for guidance and help. I can't do that. I may know what is going to happen, but I can't tell them what to do to prepare for what is going to happen, or how to avoid what is going to happen. I think you understand now."

"Yes, but it is so... so——"

"Frustrating?"

"Yes, I think so."

———

Two days later, shivering in a brisk cold breeze, they topped a low ridge on the trail and saw in a scattered wood below a large body of Indians, perhaps three hundred fifty people, mostly women and children. They wore a combination of shabby Indian and ragged white-man's clothing. Few wore coats suitable for the frigid weather. Some were astride gaunt horses, many walked, and others rode in rickety wagons pulled by poor horses.

Brett and Winona's small party walked and rode down the ridge toward the people below. When the people there saw them coming, some stopped, raised a hand in greeting. Most apparently saw the newcomers but continued moving slowly, heads hanging. The small band with Brett and Winona merged with the others and became part of the exodus.

Riding strong horses, Brett and Winnie moved slowly along the plodding line. Passing a weathered rickety wagon pulled by gaunt horses, they saw in the bed a man shrouded in blankets who looked with glazed eyes at them. A woman, sitting beside him, pulled a blanket tighter across his chest.

When they had passed the wagon, Winona looked back. "That poor man. He not look good."

"That is Chief Big Foot," said Brett. "He is sick with pneumonia. It's a very bad illness, and he needs medicine."

In the gloom, Brett and Winona sat huddled together at a small fire, watching the slick bodies of two small squirrels roasting on a spit, juices dripping on the low flames, sizzling and popping. Brett had ridden into the forest before sunset, looking for a deer to share with the others, but found only these squirrels.

Winona leaned against him. "I don't like this, Honey Brett. I don't like it. I wish we could do something for these poor people. Why is this happening to them? Why are they moving now?"

He put an arm around her shoulders. He kissed the top of her head. "Do you want me to tell you what I know?"

She hesitated, looking into the fire, turned to him. "Yes."

"The authorities, army and politicians, were very uneasy after the Little Bighorn and the widespread practice of the Ghost Dance. They know that Indians are angry and will want revenge. Even villages of peaceful Indians are being watched for any sign of trouble.

"An army force under a leader named Lt. Colonel Sumner was assigned to watch Big Foot's camp. Big Foot and Sumner actually were on good terms. They had known each other for some time and respected each other. Big Foot assured his friend Sumner that he was not going to cause trouble and had no plan to go anywhere the authorities did not want him to go.

"Now, I'm not real clear on what happens in late November and early December. I'm a little confused, never did spend much time on this period in my lectures. At some point Sumner was ordered to take Big Foot's people to Fort Meade—or was it Fort Bennett?—where they would receive their annual annuities. Big Foot seemed to be agreeable.

"Then a farmer named John Dunn, or Red Beard, who knew Big Foot well, came to the chief's camp and told him that he had heard some officers say that as soon as the Indians reached Fort Meade, the men were to be seized and taken away to prison. Dunn advised Big Foot to take his people at once to Pine Ridge where they would be in company with friendly chiefs, including Red Cloud.

"I recall that in early December, Big Foot decided to take his people to Pine Ridge where they could appeal for their annuities."

"I don't like that," said Winona. "Indian people have to go to white man's place to get food."

"I don't like it either, sweetheart. But that's the way it is, and Big Foot knows that his people will starve if he doesn't get food somewhere. Annuities at Pine Ridge seemed the best option at this point."

"Mmm. Okay, what next?"

"That is what has happened to this day, today. When I talked with Big Foot, he said we should arrive at Pine Ridge in five or six days. Then they will have food and get some new clothes, and they will be happier. And they will get medical attention. Big Foot had a very bad cold, but it became worse and progressed to pneumonia. He really needs doctors and medicines."

She bent over the fire, lifted the roasting stick and pushed the two small carcasses from the stick onto a flat stone. "Maybe we get some food at Pine Ridge, too. If they don't give food to white man, I give you some of mine." She smiled.

———

Next morning, Brett and Winona could sympathize with their companions more than usual. Like most of the Indians, they had nothing for breakfast. Brett planned to ride ahead, determined to find game that he could share.

He was still working on the horse's hobbles when he saw a band of about twenty people shuffling toward the camp. Some rode poor horses, but most walked, slowly, shuffling. The people in the camp went to them, helping them, carrying some of their meager belongings, saying they wished they had food for them. The newcomers dismounted from horses, climbed down from rickety wagons, all almost collapsing from fatigue and hunger. Winona joined the others in doing what they could for the new arrivals.

Winona went to Brett who held the reins of his horse, watching. "They so hungry and tired. They say they been moving many days, trying to stay away from soldiers."

"They are followers of Sitting Bull."

"Yes." She frowned. "How..." She shook her head. "They ran from agency after he was killed. They think soldiers want kill them, too."

"Do what you can," he said. "I will hunt today. Two men with rifles have said they will go with me." He touched her cheek, kissed her. Mounting, he rode to the edge of camp where the two young men astride gaunt ponies, waited for him. One led a third horse carrying a small pack. The three hunters rode together on a trail that led toward a wooded hillside.

———

In early evening, the three hunters returned to a boisterous welcome of shouts and cries. Two deer carcasses were strapped to the packhorse. Winona waved to Brett who returned the wave and smiled as they rode to the center of the camp. Women rushed to the packhorse, unstrapped the deer and fell to work butchering the carcasses.

Brett rode back to Winona. He dismounted slowly, stretched his back. "You were lucky today," she said, kissing him. "Honey, people say ten other men hunt today and not kill anything."

He shook his head. "Our kills will give little more than a taste to the people most in need. Some will get nothing. We'll go out again tomorrow." He led the horse to their fire circle, began unsaddling. He turned to see a woman coming, holding out two chunks of venison to Winnie.

Winnie took one piece, said something to the woman who nodded, turned, and walked away, still holding one of the meat chunks.

He went to her. "You are a good woman, my little sweetheart honey." He touched her cheek and kissed her.

"They need it more than we do. We hungry, they starving. I said take both pieces, but she would not." Winona put the venison on a flat rock at the fire circle and set to work making a fire. He unrolled their blankets, sat on them and watched her.

What now? If we stay with these people, we may starve with them. If we go away, will we ever be able to live with ourselves?

Winona pushed the chunk of meat on the spit she had fashioned as soon as the band stopped for the night, hoping she would find a use for it. She sat up, turned to see Brett who sat, eyes closed, rocking slowly back and forth.

"You okay?"

He reached over and pulled her to him. "If I didn't have you, sweetheart, I don't think I would ever be okay. Lately I wonder each night what the next day will bring. That's when I reach over to touch you. Have you noticed?"

"Yes. Sometime in moonlight, I can see you. Sometime you look very sad."

He put a hand on her cheek and pulled her to him. "Yes, sometimes I am very sad. Because I know what is going to happen to these people. But I don't know what is going to happen to me. To us."

She put her arms around him and held him.

———

Next morning, as the band was breaking camp, making ready for the trail, two riders galloped in, reined up at the fire circle where Big Foot sat cross-legged, huddled in his blankets, leaning toward the fire. Winona and Brett strolled toward the group.

The men dismounted quickly and spoke rapidly to Big Foot. The chief nodded, said something to the men who withdrew. Big Foot spoke to the woman who stood behind him. She helped him stand, and they waited.

Winona spoke softly to Brett. "They say Colonel Sumner coming. They say he not look happy. Big Foot say he will speak with Sumner. Brett, chief is very sick, very weak. He can hardly stand." Brett nodded.

A few minutes later, Sumner and four soldiers rode into camp. They dismounted, and Sumner walked to Big Foot. The chief, unsmiling, greeted him, and they sat at the fire circle, a woman helping the chief sit down. The soldiers stood aside, holding reins, talking softly, watching and listening. Winona and Brett stood nearby, but within hearing distance.

Sumner was grim. "Chief, you said you were a friend and would cause no trouble. But I hear now that you have welcomed into your camp followers of Sitting Bull. Why do you do this?"

Big Foot inhaled deeply, slowly, nodding. He spoke softly, hurting. "These are our people. They do nothing wrong. They are confused and try to find a place where they can live in peace. Before they came here, they went to Badlands, but troops there turned them back. They wandered for days before they found our camp.

"They were hungry and suffering from the cold when they came to us. They had no warm clothes. Some were almost naked. What would you do if some of your people in this condition came to you for help? Would you turn them away?"

Sumner shook his head. "We are not talking about me; we are talking about you. Sitting Bull's people are angry. They want revenge for what happened to their chief. By allowing them to come to your camp, and because people in your camp continue to do the Ghost Dance, my superiors will call you an enemy. I don't like this, old friend, but I am a soldier, and I follow orders. I have troops camped near here. We will escort you to Pine Ridge."

Big Foot nodded. "Yes, we go to Pine Ridge."

Brett turned to go, and Winona followed. They stopped at their hobbled horses and looked back at the chief and Sumner. "Winnie, I know how you feel about these people, but we should not go with them."

"Why? I want to help them. I want to go."

"Remember when you said you didn't like it when the cosmic-thing takes us somewhere when we could be trying to go to another place where bad things are not happening?"

"I remember, but these people are almost to Pine Ridge where they will get food and clothing and be inside where they will be warm. I want to see them happy. I want to go. Then we will go to another place, just you and me, and we won't listen to cos-thing. Please."

He looked into her eyes, put his hands on her cheeks and kissed her. He went to his horse, bent, and checked the hobbles.

CHAPTER 11

B rett and Winona stood beside their horses, reins tied to a shrub. They stared at the wagon where Big Foot lay, covered in blood-spattered blankets. A white flag fluttered on a staff attached to the side of the wagon. An army officer stood beside the wagon, talking with Big Foot. A dozen soldiers stood nearby, chatting, smoking, holding their horses' reins.

"That would be Major Whitside," Brett said. "He and his superiors consider Big Foot and his people dangerous, especially since they welcomed Sitting Bull's followers. Whitside has relieved Sumner and will deal with Big Foot now. When news came to Big Foot that Whitside had ridden into camp, he sent word to the major that he would like to talk.

"Whitside went to him and told him that talking was finished. He must surrender, and his troops will escort the chief and his band to the army's camp at a place called Wounded Knee. Big Foot agreed. He has no choice. He has a village of cold and hungry people, including but a hundred weakened warriors.

"Big Foot likely was also influenced by messages he recently received from Pine Ridge. A number of chiefs there reported to him that other bands had surrendered and were coming to the agency. Big Foot will realize by now that he and his people are captives. But at least, even as captives, they will eventually reach Pine Ridge."

"Why are they captives? They have done nothing wrong. They do what they supposed to do, go to agency for annuities."

"Authorities will say they danced the Ghost Dance too long, and they welcomed Sitting Bull's people to their camp. This makes them dangerous people in their eyes. Stupid. Look at them. They are not a danger to anyone."

————

In the gloaming following sunset, the column of rickety wagons and horses, surrounded by soldiers, rode down the slope and across the wooden planks of Wounded Knee bridge. The column passed the tiny post office and, across the road, Mousseau's store. Here the column paused as Indians rushed into the store to buy candles, sugar, coffee, other supplies they had not seen in months. Their money quickly exhausted, they resumed their progress to a shallow ravine where Whitside ordered the Indians to set up their camp.

"Look, honey," Winona said. Brett and Winona had followed the Indians to their assigned site. Soldiers and Indians were putting up five large tents. Winona talked with a woman who stood with them, watching. The woman said that a stove was going to be put into the tent assigned to Big Foot, and the army doctor was coming to examine him. Winona smiled broadly. She said that the major had ordered bacon and hardtack issued to the Indians.

"That so good," Winona said, "and when they reach agency, everything will be even better."

"That is quite true." Winnie and Brett were startled by the officer who had walked up behind them.

"Sorry, didn't mean to butt in." The lieutenant smiled. "My boss asked me to find out who you two are. The Indians seem to be quite at ease with you. Can't say the same about their attitude toward us."

"Ah. I'm Brett Davis. I'm a... freelance reporter writing about these people who appear to be giving up their wild ways and going to a settled existence at the agency." He motioned toward Winona. "This is Winona, my interpreter. She speaks English and half a dozen Indian languages."

The lieutenant looked longer than necessary at Winona. She turned aside. He looked back to Brett. "Freelance, you say. Well, the major likes to keep the public informed. He will probably want to talk to you when he has the time. I suppose you have noted that he is pretty busy at the moment. What newspapers do you sell to?"

Brett frowned. "Ah, well, uh, any newspaper who will pay me for the story. I've sold to *Dallas Morning News*, uh, *Atlanta Journal*, *Albuquerque Journal*." *Shouldn't have said Atlanta Journal. Judging from his accent, he's obviously a southerner.*

"Have you met Mr. Tibbles? He's a reporter for an Omaha newspaper." Brett shook his head. "I'll tell him about you. He'll look you up. Be sure you have time on your hands. He asks a lotta questions."

The lieutenant looked anxiously back toward the woods behind the Indian camp. "Gotta go now. Things gettin' interesting. Get your pen and paper out." The lieutenant nodded to Brett, looked quickly at Winona before turning and striding toward the woods.

Brett looked into the woods. The cavalry camp was set up in the trees a hundred yards from the Indian camp. As the lieutenant strode toward the wood, soldiers began to file from the camp, moving into place, completely surrounding the Indian camp in minutes. Brett searched the hillside and saw what he was looking for. Two Hotchkiss guns pointed directly at the Indian camp.

She saw the guns. "What is it?"

"They are a special kind of gun. They fire many shots, very fast, and the bullets explode when they hit something."

"Why are they putting those guns up there? The Indians are not doing anything wrong."

"The Indians are prisoners. The army does not trust them."

They started at the sound of approaching horses. In the evening gloom, they saw a long column of riders coming in. "That will be soldiers of the Seventh Cavalry under Colonel Forsyth coming in to support Whitside's force," Brett said. "Remember the Seventh Cavalry, the force under Custer? The soldiers of the Seventh Cav do not like Indians." *It's unlikely that any of the common soldiers in this bunch were at the Little Bighorn, but some of the officers were there with Forsyth.*

It doesn't matter, of course, who was there or not there.
Unit pride and memory run strong and long.

Brett recalled the figures that had always impressed him. Forsyth and Whitside now had 470 troopers to watch 340 Indians in poor condition, in spite of the bacon and hardtack, of whom only 106 were warriors. The great majority of the Indian people were women and children.

"Look." Winnie pointed at the two Hotchkiss guns in the column.

"Yes, they will be installed beside the two guns there." He pointed to the hillside above the Indian camp.

Lanterns in the army camp, and fires in the army and Indian camps soon burned down, and the camps slept. Brett remembered from the histories that the officers in the army camp were the last to retire. They had celebrated the capture of Big Foot and his people with a small keg of whiskey sent by the Pine Ridge storekeeper.

———

First light. Brett stood beside his blanket, watched the eastern horizon brighten and color the lacy cloud layers shades of pink, red and purple. A light breeze touched his cheeks, not like the frigid wind yesterday, but mild, forecasting a pleasant day.

He bent over the fire pit, stirred the ashes of last night's fire, found some live embers and dropped small dry sticks on the glow. They erupted into tiny flames, and he dropped larger sticks on the fire. He put his hands over the flames, rubbed them together.

From their campsite on a slope just above the Indian camp, Brett looked across the square below to the hillside opposite to see soldiers moving into position. They had withdrawn yesterday at dusk, but now resumed their positions surrounding the Indian camp.

He went to the horses, saddled them, and led them slowly to a tree where he tied the reins. He was working on the hobbles when Winona threw back her blanket and went quickly to the fire, squatted and extended her hands over the low flames. She saw him at the horses.

"Why you saddle horses so early?" she said.

He didn't answer, looked over his horse's back, jiggled the horn, checking the tightness of the cinch.

"Honey?"

He walked to her. "We should leave now. This is not going to be a good day."

She looked up at him. "What you mean? It will be a good day. Woman yesterday say we reach Pine Ridge today in just a few hours. This a good day. I want to go with these people." She stiffened, chin raised. "I *will* go." She softened. "*We* will go." She frowned, then a hint of a smile, a hopeful smile.

He set his jaw, said nothing. He looked around the camp below that was now awake, women working on a breakfast of more bacon and hardtack, men loading wagons. Children ran about the camp, darting among the lodges and tents, laughing and playing as they had not in many moons.

Brett shook his head violently. *What to do? How can I convince Winnie that we cannot stay?* He looked around the camp below and up the slope opposite. Soldiers lounged on the hills and flats, surrounding the Indian camp, chatting and smoking.

What can I say to her without telling her the brutal truth?

His head jerked up at the sound of the bugle. *Officer's Call.* He knew the call from reenactments he had done. Now he saw soldiers below and on slopes above the Indian camp quickly drop smokes, stand tall and face the camp, awaiting orders from officers, now receiving their own orders from the colonel.

Too late! Dammit! Too late.

"Good morning!" Bret jumped, turned to see the lieutenant they had talked with yesterday walking toward them. Brett nodded. "Just wanted to brief you on what's going on today. We're going to collect the Indians' guns this morning. We don't expect every buck to have a rifle, but most will. Some of the boys have seen their guns, and they're actually better armed than we are. They have Winchester twelve-shot repeaters; we have single-shot Remingtons. I hope they don't know that." He snorted. "They're probably more experienced in using guns than our boys, too.

"Most of our boys are inexperienced, and some are raw recruits, in the army no more'n a month. Some of 'em from the city slums never even *saw* a horse till they joined up. Anyhow, we have the bucks outnumbered four to one, and we're satisfied with a show of force rather than fighting.

"I don't know who the officers are going to be talking with this mornin'. I saw the chief earlier—I'm detailed to help the doctor who's lookin' after him—and he is one sick fellow. He's got a stove in his tent, and he's all wrapped up in blankets, and a scarf tied over his head, and he's still shiverin'. He cain't hardly sit up.

"Shouldn't be telling you all this. Don't put it in

your piece. The Colonel would not be happy with you. Or me." He pulled a face. "Just report what happens. Gonna be an interesting day." He held up an arm in goodbye. "I expect all will go well," he said over his shoulder, "but you watch out for yourselves, and take care, hear?"

Winona moved to Brett who stared down at the Indian camp. "It's starting," he said softly. He looked eastward and saw through the forest canopy the sun just clearing the horizon. He started at the sound of the bugle, frowned. *That would be...can't remember the name, but it's the call to the troops to gather around their immediate officer for final orders.*

As if in answer to his own pondering, troops every-where crowded around officers, then disbursed quickly to assigned positions. The Indian camp was surrounded again, and lines of support fanned out in many direc-tions. A mounted troop took up position a short distance from the camp.

From their position on a gentle slope above the center of the Indian camp, Brett and Winona had a good view of the camp and the lines of troops surrounding it. Brett shook his head. *Stupid. Should be obvious to anybody, trained in military tactics or unaware of military tactics, that if troops were to fire on the Indians within the encircled camp, they inevitably would hit soldiers on the other side of the camp.*

In fact, he recalled reading that T. H. Tibbles, the *Omaha World* reporter, had reached the same conclu-sion. While the Indians were gathering below, Tibbles had wandered up to the Hotchkiss gun positions above the camp and raised the question with the officer in charge there. *Captain Ilsey, is it?* The captain laughed and said there would be no trouble and no shooting.

"Simple," he said. "Big Foot wants to take his people to the agency, and we're happy to be their escort. What could be simpler and more peaceable than that?"

"Listen," Winona said. They heard singing. "That is camp crier, walking around the lodges, singing about the army officer calling men to come to center of camp near Big Foot tent for a council." They saw men casually walking from lodges to the camp center. There they stood and sat, smoking, talking, laughing.

As Forsyth, Whitside and an interpreter walked toward the gathering, the people moved aside, making way, and conversation ended. Forsyth then spoke, and the interpreter repeated his words in Lakota. Winnie strained to hear and interpreted for Brett.

Forsyth spoke softly, smiling, explaining that all is well. "Everyone is safe now, the soldiers are your friends, rations have been increased, and no one will be hungry." He turned serious. "At the same time, we must remember that there have been troubles in the past, and there could still be some bad people among all these good people here, so we're going to prevent anything bad happening by asking you to give up your guns."

The Indian men looked at each other, frowning, whispering, murmuring. This was something they had not expected.

"What will they do?" Winona said. "I think there could be trouble. Indian men believe they have a right to own bows and guns. They have never been asked to give them up."

"Yes," Brett said. "There could be trouble." He knew that the Indians had agreed to submit to the soldiers, but to ask a brave to give up his weapon was to ask him to give up his manhood. Even if he had no intention of using the weapon. Adding to their apprehension, the Indian men had heard stories about Indians willingly giving up their weapons to white men who then shot them dead.

The Indian men chose two men to go into Big Foot's tent to ask his guidance.

Brett recalled from the histories the conversation that passed between Big Foot and the two men. Big Foot told them to give the soldiers some bad guns, but keep the good ones. Forsyth's interpreter, who had followed the two men into the chief's tent, urged them to surrender all their guns. You can replace the guns, he said, but if there is trouble, you can't replace a man who is killed. Big Foot was unmoved. He vowed they would keep the good guns.

The two men and the interpreter came out and said nothing. Forsyth waited only a moment. He proceeded with a plan that he undoubtedly had prepared, expecting no cooperation. He selected twenty Indian men from the group and instructed them to go to the lodges, collect all the guns, and bring them to him. The men left the circle and returned shortly, carrying only two broken old rifles that a lieutenant quipped were useful only as children's toys.

Whitside, more experienced in dealing with Indians than Forsyth, told the Colonel that he knew the Indians had many modern rifles in good condition. At his suggestion, Forsyth had Big Foot brought out from his tent. The chief had worsened, now bleeding from his nose and shaking. Forsyth asked the chief to tell his men to deliver their guns. Big Foot replied that they had no guns. Soldiers at the last agency where they had called, he said, had taken all their guns and burned them.

Whitside and Forsyth changed tactics. They organized two groups of soldiers and sent them to each end of the Indian camp. They would search the lodges and tents for guns and work toward each other, ending at the camp center.

Brett and Winnie watched the two details move out and begin their search. Because the Indians were jumpy, on the point of anger, it was going to be a sensitive operation. Following directions, only officers entered lodges and tents while troopers searched outside. The enlisted men angered Indians by shoving contents from wagons to the ground, opening packs and confiscating knives, axes, hatchets, needles, anything that could be considered a weapon. They searched women who were sometimes found sitting on a rifle or concealing one under her skirts.

Winona pointed to an officer who walked casually among the women, talking with them. The women laughed with him, enjoying the distraction from the treatment they were enduring from the other soldiers. The officer played with children and stroked babies' cheeks. He spoke and joked with the men who sat, smoking and chatting, enjoying the mild winter sun.

"Does he do that to make people forget what is happening," said Winona, "or is he a good man?"

"Who knows?" Brett said. "I think he is a good man. Maybe he doesn't like what is happening to the people and wants to make it as easy as possible."

Winona took Brett's arm. "Honey Brett, something gonna happen." He nodded. They saw an unmistakable change in the mood of the gathering. Many in the crowd, especially among the young men, began to be agitated. They glared at the soldiers ringing the camp, rifles in hand. Their faces turned anxious, leaning to anger, as they paced, talking softly.

Big Foot saw the growing uneasiness and asked to be raised from his bed so he could urge calm. He tried to speak, but he was so weak, no one seemed to hear him, and he collapsed on his bed.

God, why do you let this happen? If you are the divine arbiter, as I was taught, why do you do this?

"Look, there is Yellow Bird, the medicine man!" said Winona. "I met him yesterday. He was so unhappy, so down, so, how you say..."

"Depressed?"

"Yes, depressed. He say his people are going to die if they go on like they have been going for so long. He say they must remember the old ways and return there."

While she spoke, Yellow Bird, painted and feathered, rose and extended his arms. He spoke loudly, calling the people to listen. Everyone in hearing stopped what they were doing and listened.

Winona translated. "He pray that ghost shirts protect the warriors." She looked anxiously at Brett. "Uh-oh."

Then Yellow Bird danced in a circle, blowing on a whistle. He bent to grab handfuls of dust that he threw into the air. He stopped, faced the young men, and shouted: "Ahan!"

"That mean 'look out, something bad gonna happen,'" Winona said.

Then Yellow Bird cried in a strong voice: "I have lived long enough!"

Winona turned to Brett, wide-eyed. "That what warriors say just before going into a fight."

The Indian men crowded around Yellow Bird who continued, as if in a trance. He urged the warriors to be strong and not be afraid. The soldiers' bullets would not penetrate their shirts. The bullets would fly over them to the wide prairie, just as the dust he threw up had floated away in the wind.

The Indians shouted in reply, "Hau! Hau!"

Winona grabbed handfuls of Brad's shirt, looked up at him. "That mean 'amen' or 'we believe you.' I don't like it."

Forsyth and the others standing with him had watched all this. Forsyth turned to a lieutenant behind him. "That man is a troublemaker. Tell him to sit down and be quiet." The lieutenant went to Yellow Bird and spoke to him. The medicine man seemed surprised at the command, but he stopped dancing, backed up, and sat on the ground. The young men standing nearby glared at the lieutenant but did nothing.

The search party returned to the circle. They carried armloads of axes, knives, metal bars and crowbars, and dumped the lot in a pile in the square. On top of the pile, they deposited all the rifles they found, thirty-eight, mostly old pieces that appeared to be useless. Only a few were the modern repeating Winchesters.

"Winnie, we must leave now," Brett said. "I have packed everything, and we need to go. Now."

She leaned back, frowning. "No, I want to see. Everything is okay. The people are doing what the army wants them to do."

"Forsyth and the other officers are not pleased. It is going to be bad, very bad. Will you go now?"

She turned to him, grim. "Brett. I tell you. I am *not* going! I want to see this. I want to go to agency with the people. You leave if you want. I find you later. I stay!" She turned her back to him.

He slumped. *If I carry her away bodily, she will never forgive me. Maybe after learning what happens, but...*

Brett was not surprised by Whitside's response to the results of the search. The colonel said he knew that the Indians have modern rifles. Just yesterday, the men had proudly showed the soldiers their repeating Winchesters.

Since the searchers had not found the rifles in or outside the lodges, Whitside decided they must have the rifles hidden on their bodies under blankets. He spoke loudly: "This will not do! We know you have modern rifles. Now, I do not wish to insult you with a personal search of your bodies, so I am asking all the men to step forward, remove your blankets and give up your weapons."

A group of older men stepped forward and opened their blankets to show they had no guns. At that instant, Yellow Bird jumped up and commenced dancing and chanting before the young men, none of whom had come forward.

The commander sent a half dozen soldiers into the circle and ordered the Indians to come forward. Three Indians, looking around nervously, stepped up and opened their blankets. Two held rifles.

At that moment, an angry young man jumped up, pulled a Winchester from beneath his blanket, raised it high over his head, and began to dance in circles. He shouted that this was his gun, and he was not about to surrender it to anyone unless they paid him for it. Yellow Bird jumped up. He danced and whirled, chanting, blowing a whistle and tossing dirt over his head. He urged the men to be strong and remember the ghost shirts would protect them from an enemy's bullets. Another medicine man sprang up and began singing a ghost dance song. Winona interpreted, her voice breaking as she looked anxiously at Brett.

All the young Indians now stood, milled about, confused, tense, drifting away from the soldiers who waited to collect their guns. They pulled their blankets tight around their bodies.

Soldiers bordering the square tensed. Most had never seen violent action beyond street brawls before they donned a uniform. Most had never fired a weapon except at a target. Now they gripped their rifles tightly, glancing nervously at the officers.

Winona squeezed Brett's arm, looking anxiously at him. "What is happening? Something bad. Should we go?"

"Too late now. Both sides below are so jumpy, they may shoot at anything that moves. We stay. Here, let's move very slowly behind the two trees there." He motioned with a nod to two heavy-trunked trees that they inched behind. They leaned against the trees. Winona peered around her tree, but Brett pushed her back.

"No. Stay hidden. There is nothing we can do."

At that instant, a rifle shot sounded below, followed by another, and another. Then a burst of rifle fire, followed by the unmistakable explosive sound of the

Hotchkiss guns firing. Shouts and anguished cries rose below. Winona slid down the trunk to sit on the ground. She covered her face with both hands.

"Stay behind your tree! Don't look!" Brett shouted.

She rocked back and forth, tears streaming through her fingers. The firing below continued, a single rifle shot, a volley of rifle shots, the rattling fire of the Hotchkiss guns, all mingled with the anguished shouts and cries of injured and frightened people, Indians and soldiers alike. Then a lull, then a volley of rifle shots from a distance. Then more firing from below, accompanied by shouts and cries from soldiers and Indians and the screaming of women and children.

Brett's and Winona's horses, reins tied to a low branch nearby, shied at the shots, snorted, quieted, jerked against the reins at another volley.

Brett jumped when a bullet struck the tree trunk that shielded him. Then another thunk of a bullet striking the trunk. "Stay behind your tree, Winnie! We're getting some stray shots!" He slid down the trunk and sat down hard, his back against the tree.

She leaned against the trunk, hugging her knees, rocking back and forth. "Sorry. I so sorry. I did not know. I did not want see this. Sorry, sorry."

He spoke softly. "It's okay, Winnie. It was going to happen, whether we were here or not. Just stay behind your tree."

They listened, cowering behind the tree trunks. The firing below diminished to an occasional shot, then quiet, a shot, then silence but for the moans and cries of the wounded and shouted orders of the officers.

Cease fire, an officer yelled. Stop shooting, called

another. For God's sake, said another, stop shooting at them!

Brett struggled to stand, stretched and flexed his back. *How long had it been? An hour? A day? A lifetime? I have lost all perception of time.* Peering around the trunk, he looked below. He shuddered, seeing what he expected to see. He had read about it, taught it. Now he saw it.

Bodies of Indians and soldiers lay strewn about the square and among the tents and lodges. Many of the lodges were destroyed, some gutted, some burned, struck by the exploding Hotchkiss shells. There were bodies, warriors and soldiers, but most were women and children. Soldiers moved about, bending, looking for wounded, calling for help.

Brett went to Winona. She sat, leaning against the tree, hands covering her face. He touched her shoulder. She lowered her hands, looked up.

"I so sorry, Brett, honey Brett. I must listen to you. If I don't listen to you, hit me."

He smiled thinly. "If I ever hit you, shoot me." She took his hand in both of hers and pressed it to her cheek, tried to smile and choked back a sob.

"I'm going below," he said.

She withdrew her hands, rested them in her lap. "I stay here. I don't want see. It is like... like the end of my people, the end of our way. I don't want to see."

He bent to a knee, took her face in his hands, and kissed her. "I won't be long. Then we'll go. We'll find a good place. I promise. No more cosmic thing."

She didn't look at him, stared at her hands in her lap. "I don't think I ever see a good place again. Not for me."

He stood, looked aside to the forest, green, still, inviting. From a grassy, sun-splashed clearing, the sweet trill of a meadowlark.

We will find a good place, Winnie and I.

"Stay here then. I won't be long." He touched her head.

He walked down the slope to the square below. Soldiers were carrying the wounded, Indians and soldiers, from the square to wagons where they would be transported to a field hospital that was at that moment already being set up. He was ignored by the soldiers as he walked among the corpses, shaking his head at the carnage. If he remembered correctly, at least one hundred seventy Indians, two-thirds of them women and children, and twenty-five soldiers died that day.

Other wagons were loaded with dead soldiers. The bodies would be transported to burial in consecrated ground. The Indian bodies were left where they fell.

Brett stopped when he saw the unmistakable body of Big Foot. The chief lay on his back, dried blood on his forehead from a bullet hole. The corpse of a woman lay across his body. *That would be his daughter, shot in the back as she ran to him.*

He looked around the square and to the lodges beyond where soldiers collected corpses. He shook his head. *What a waste. What a damned waste. Why have human beings devised such efficient ways to destroy each other?*

Brett noticed two soldiers who had just hoisted a body between them stop to look curiously at him. He decided it was time to withdraw. He nodded to the men, went to the slope, and walked up to Winona.

But Winona was not there. *She must be doing her business.* "Winnie," he called softly. No answer. "Winnie!" Still no answer. He thrashed about in the bushes. Nothing. Both horses were still tied where he had left them.

He walked slowly around the clearing where they had camped to watch the action below. The ground was hardpacked in the clearing, but covered with dry leaves under trees and shrubs. *There!* He bent to examine faint footprints in the dead leaves between low shrubs. Pushing through the shrubs, he found hoofprints of two horses. He went to his horses, untied reins and mounted, leading Winona's horse.

He followed the hoofprints slowly, kicking his horse to a lope when the prints showed more distinctly on clear dry ground.

————

In the gloom at dusk, a new campfire burned brightly. A young man stood beside tethered horses, looking back at his pard who stood facing Winona. She sat on the ground, leaning against a tree, looking aside.

"You thank we gotta tie her up, or just hang on to 'er?" said the man facing Winona.

"I don't know. Never done this before?"

The man frowned. "You never done it before?" He snorted. The boy at the horses shook his head.

"You come on over here. You be first. I'm gonna enjoy watching this." He laughed.

The boy grinned. He walked over, stood in front of Winnie. He unbuttoned his pants, pushed them down.

"That's enough. Playtime's over, boys."

The men jerked around to see Brett step from the darkness, his pistol leveled on them. The boy pulled his pants up, stretched his arms high, and the pants slid to his ankles.

"For god's sake, pull up your pants," said Brett. The boy quickly obeyed, buttoning the pants, then hoisted his hands high.

The other man glared at Brett. His hand hovered over his holster.

Brett turned his six-shooter on the man. "Actually, I'd like you to do that so I can put a hole in your head and be done with it. Haven't you seen enough bloodshed for a lifetime? I saw you two back at Wounded Knee."

"We ain't soldiers," said the boy nervously. "We're teamsters, working for the army." His arms still reached for the sky.

"Then you should be back at Wounded Knee, working for the army." He shook his head. "Put your arms down." The boy lowered his arms, almost smiled nervously.

Winona stood and walked to Brett. Her face was blank. "You okay?" he said. She nodded.

"If I'd rode up on you ten minutes later, boys, you'd both be dead now." The two men looked at each other. "Now I want you to do your duty and ride back to Wounded Knee."

"Now?" said the older man.

"Now," Brett said. "If they shoot you in the dark, that's your problem. Now, git!"

The men strode to their horses, almost running. They swung into the saddle and galloped away.

"Do you think they go to Wounded Knee?" she said.

"Nah, they would be crazy to go there."

They walked into the darkness where he had left the horses. He untied the reins and offered Winnie hers.

She ignored the reins and put her arms around him, holding him tightly, resting her head on his chest. "Brett honey. What we do now? Where we go? We only go bad places. Is there no happy place we can go?"

"I swear, if there is a happy place on the globe, anywhere, we will go there. I promise."

———

In the bright moonlight, they rode on the back trail to a small stream he had crossed while looking for Winona. Shivering, they built a hasty campfire, wrapped in their blankets and huddled against each other in the frigid late December night, staring into the dancing flames.

He pondered, remembering what he had read about the aftermath of the fighting at Wounded Knee. When word of the fighting reached Pine Ridge, some warriors who some time ago had left the Badlands to surrender to authorities at the agency now rode to Wounded Knee and attacked soldiers who were still tending to survivors and collecting army dead. It was a short anti-climax for the group of angry warriors were no match for the army numbers.

The Indian dead lay on the field for days after the end of the battle, frozen and contorted. Some bodies were almost naked. Souvenir hunters had wandered among the corpses, taking anything they found interesting. The souvenir ghouls were particularly interested in ghost shirts.

Brett shuddered at the memory of the iconic photograph of Big Foot. Wearing an overcoat, scarf wrapped around his head, lying on the ground, his shoulders raised off the ground, as if trying to rise, frozen rigid, eyes open and staring upward, as if searching eternity for answers. Brett closed his eyes, shuddered again. The photograph had haunted him since he first saw it. He saw the body today and knew this reality would never leave him.

He recalled reading that the Indian corpses would not be buried until New Year's Day, if "buried" is the appropriate term. Bodies were tumbled into a long pit without any ceremony by priests who had labored hard to minister to them when living.

It's over. Finally, it's over.

While Winona rolled out their blankets, Brett built up the fire, piled more tinder near the fire circle and climbed into the bed, shivering.

She came to the bed, pulled up the covers, and snuggled against him. "I love you, honey," she said.

He kissed the tip of her nose. "I love you, sweetheart." He reached around her, pulled her to him, feeling her body warm against his. He kissed her cheek, her neck, ran his hand down her back, pulled her close.

She kissed his lips, leaned back. "What is 'globe'?"

CHAPTER 12

Brett was awakened by distant birdsong. His eyes still closed, he listened. Chip, chip, cheep, chip. *I think... yes...Western Bluebird.* He opened his eyes, pushed the cover down and sat up. He saw the top of the sun ball that had just appeared at the eastern horizon, coloring the sky above bright golden.

He looked around. "There's Buddy, my old buddy." His horse, hobbled nearby on a patch of grass, bobbed his head up and down, snorting.

Beyond the horse, tall Timothy Grass in the dry pasture swayed in the light breeze. *Appears to be just about ready for cutting. This farmer should have a good hay crop.* Pulling on his boots, he stood and buttoned his jeans. He walked to the stream. About ten feet wide, dry leaves and a couple of candy wrappers floated in the languid stream. Across the creek, a dozen Angus and Hereford cattle grazed on the rolling grassland. *Alfalfa, I think.*

He picked up the saddle that had served as a hard pillow, went to the horse and saddled up. He wasn't bothered by the rifle and scabbard. They were gone. After tightening the cinch, he rummaged in the saddle bags and pulled out his wallet. He confirmed that the wallet contained a few greenbacks, Federal Reserve Notes. He put the wallet in his jeans pocket and searched the saddle bags again. No pistol, no cartridges.

Picking up the thin blanket, he shook it, rolled it and stuffed it into a saddlebag. He bridled the horse, removed hobbles and stuffed them into saddlebags. He stood beside the horse a moment, his fist on the saddle horn, looking around.

He mounted, pointed the horse toward the county park, and set out at a lope.

———

Professor Davis walked into the classroom from the hall and went to the table at the front. Most students were seated, fussing with backpacks, putting away cell-phones, pulling out notepads and iPads. A few were standing, talking, when Davis came in. Seeing him, they went to their seats, sat down, and faced front.

Davis leaned on the lectern, waiting. Conversation in the room diminished and ended. He straightened, smiled. "I hope your weekend was as rewarding as mine."

"What did you do?" said Thomas, sitting in his usual chair in the back row.

The professor pondered a moment, looked to the windows, searching. He turned back to the class. "I went... camping. Good for the soul, camping, if you can find a solitary place where you are interrupted only by birdsong in the morning and coyotes at night."

He looked again at the open window, studied the leaves fluttering in the soft breeze. "If you know a place where you can find peace... where you can dream." He stared long at the window. Students glanced uneasily at each other, beginning to fidget.

He turned back to the class. He smiled. "Now—"

The hall door opened. A young, pretty woman, clad in a buckskin dress decorated with tassels and beads, wearing moccasins, walked through the door. She went to Davis's desk, looking only at him, and stopped beside him. She placed a breastplate of buckskin, thin bones and tassels on the desk, then turned to face the room.

Students smiled, frowned, whispered, stared at the woman.

"Class," said Brett, "this is Winona."

Epilogue

B rett sat at a researcher's table at the National Archives, bent over the stack of documents he had just pulled from a dusty box. He was in the closing stages of the manuscript he had worked on for the two years since his retirement from teaching. He was determined, rather pompously, he admitted, to write the definitive history of the end of the plains Indian wars. Why not definitive? He was there. He knew exactly what happened. He saw it.

He shook his head slowly. He knew that seeing what happened with his own eyes proved nothing. Lieutenant Matthew Avers with the Seventh Cav contingent also saw what happened at Wounded Knee with his own eyes, and the account of the engagement included in his memoir published in 1905 could not have been more different from Brett's recollection.

Avers described it as a magnificent victory, finally putting an end to the opposition of the savages to progress settling the great plains. Brett had long since determined that he would not be influenced by Avers and other participants who wrote their own versions of what happened.

He was focusing now on the events that led to the unrest at Standing Rock Agency and the death of Sitting Bull. He read a faded letter from Major McLaughlin, the agent at Standing Rock, to General Miles, thanking the General for his letter commending the agent for his handling of the "Sitting Bull affair". Brett shook his head. He had never thought of Sitting Bull's demise as an "affair", rather cold-blooded murder.

He leafed through documents slowly, reading enough to decide that the piece was not relevant to his story.

Then he stopped, bent over a sheaf of a dozen or so pages, held together by a string laced through two holes. He held the hand-written document up to the light from the window. The top of the first page was dated January 23, 1932, Boonton, New Jersey. Below the date, the document was headed: "A personal account of the Mission of William F. Cody to the Standing Rock Agency in respect to Sitting Bull".

Brett read the first page, and there it was. At the bottom of that first page, there was a reference to the writer standing with Cody, talking with a white man, a reporter from the *Dallas Morning News*. Standing beside this white man, said the document, was a young, pretty Indian woman.

Brett leaned back, smiling a hint of a smile. He looked toward the window. "Winnie, c'mere." She stepped around the end of a rack loaded with boxes. "Look at this," he said, pointing to the text he had just read. She rested a hand on his shoulder and leaned over to look at the paper.

"This is proof," he said. "I was there."

If You Liked This, You Might Enjoy: Along Came Jenny

BEST-SELLING AUTHOR HARLAN HAGUE RETURNS WITH WESTERN ROMANCE AT ITS FINEST—SUBTLE AND THOUGHT-PROVOKING.

Josh Nesbitt returns to Texas from service in the Civil War a broken man, and—for the first time in his life—he's imagining the unthinkable. But then he meets Jenny Weston, a full-of-life cook who enjoys the occasional cattle drive.

As Josh and Jenny set out on a drive beset by storms, stampedes, rustlers and Indians who think they own the land and cattle cross, Josh starts to believe in the possibility of a life not shrouded in painful war memories.

But when their cattle drive nears an end in Abilene, Kansas, the question remains ... will Josh and Jenny decide to plant roots once and for all?

Along Came Jenny tells a story full of good conversation around evening campfires, stories and jokes, real and imaginary tales, desperation and sadness, and ... a life full of wonder and hope.

AVAILABLE NOW

About the Author

Harlan Hague, Ph.D., is a native Texan who has lived in Japan and England. His travels have taken him to about eighty countries and dependencies and a circumnavigation of the globe.

Hague is a prize-winning historian and award-winning novelist. History specialties are exploration and trails, California's Mexican era, American Indians, and the environment. His novels are mostly westerns with romance themes. Two novels are set largely in Japan and a novella in Belize. Some titles have been translated into Spanish, Italian, Portuguese, and German. In addition to history, biography, and fiction, he once wrote travel articles that published in newspapers around the country, and he has written a bit of fantasy. His screenplays are making the rounds.

For more information about what he has done and what he is doing, visit his website at harlanhague.us. Hague lives in California.

Made in the USA
Coppell, TX
18 November 2022